The Panic Room
and other stories

Jim Fairfax

ISBN: 9798645698249

Typeset in 10.5/14 Garamond

For Sarah

The Panic Room and other stories

CONTENTS

The Panic Room and other stories

The Priest and the Silverback

He had been a powerfully built man in his youth and a keen amateur boxer. Indeed, before he took up training for the Church there had been rumours that he could have been a professional. Sixty years on, he was still living in the same remote area of the Congo where he had been stationed for his last missionary post. Like an old cheese only suitable for flavouring soup, he had hung around too long.

For a big man, and Father O'Donoghue was big in many ways, he did not exude the stereotypical hilarity and bonhomie. In fact, he spent hours piously reciting with his rosary and on his knees praying. He had board and lodging at the mission provided, but the local diocese struggled to find a task to occupy his many hours of free time. His manner did not endear him to the local people, who viewed him as patronising and obtuse, appearing to them to speak in riddles. Then the latest curate to arrive, Father Devereaux, a handsome young Irishman with dark hair and black eyes, suggested a role for Father O'Donoghue. During each bi-weekly mass there was a collection at each of the twelve churches in the diocese; a myriad of spatially separated villages, with no specific centre. Why not give the responsibility for the gathering and transportation of all these

1

monies to Father O'Donoghue, he suggested. The bishop happily agreed, recruiting Adebayo, who helped at the mission, to provide the priest with transport.

And so the following week, the sandal-clad elderly priest could be seen with a crash helmet on his head clinging onto the back of Adebayo, as the small moped wheezed loudly as it weaved its way along the dirt tracks between the villages. The rather comical sight of the large man, shifting his weight on the seat, as his driver attempted to keep the vehicle upright, was not wasted on the locals they passed.

However, the scheme was declared a resounding success by the bishop, who was pleased to see one of his elders now more fully occupied. Of course, there were a lot of churches to visit on each trip and to give both the priest and Adebayo a comfort break, it was decided that they would stop for a half an hour at the centrally positioned village of Mopago. One of the larger villages, it possessed not just a church, but also a simple restaurant popular with locals from the surrounding areas. It was particularly appealing as it had a large indoor dining room with a fairly basic, but efficient, air conditioning system which provided much welcomed respite from the burning midday heat.

On arrival, at just after two o'clock, they found the restaurant still busy from lunchtime. Delicious aromas wafted out from kitchen at the back of the building. Adebayo parked the moped and made his way to order some food and drink. However, the priest merely asked for a glass of water and some fruit. Looking at the crowded room, he decided instead to sit on a shady bench, under a large tree on the edge of the forest opposite the building. He did not like people much and he certainly did not like crowds. Although Adebayo was a pleasant and respectful fellow, Father O'Donoghue also felt he needed a short break from his company. So he sat alone, reflecting on the day. After consuming the fruit and quenching his thirst, he turned to his rosary beads for solace. The beads were much worn and had been with the priest a very long time.

After a few minutes he became aware of a presence behind him. When he had sat down he had not paid any particular attention to the area behind the bench. It had appeared to be a small copse of trees that backed onto an area of forest. When he heard the crunch on the ground he imagined that maybe an inquisitive goat or antelope had wandered over. So he was taken aback when he turned around to see a magnificent silverback gorilla starring back at him through the small amount of thin foliage. Father O'Donoghue jumped up in alarm and in the process dropped his beloved rosary beads.

To his surprise, the silverback walked forward and picked up the beads. The round gemstone eyes gazed at the beads in awe. And then a most wonderful thing happened. The gorilla held the beads in his hands and moved them through

3

his fingers so beautifully, that the priest was mesmerised. He had never seen anybody hold the beads in such a deft way. The silverback held the beads lovingly, as they moved so dexterously through his agile fingers, rather like a tailor sewing a masterpiece. To Father O'Donoghue this felt like a near religious experience and he raised his eyes heavenwards in silent prayer. After a while the creature became aware of the man looking so intently at the beads and in a flash threw them to the ground and ambled quickly back into the depths of the forest from the clearing.

It was only when Adebayo waved over to indicate that they needed to continue on their journey, that the priest came out of his trance and realised that he was meant to be guarding the takings. Looking down he was relieved to see that the large brown satchel that held the monies was still next to where he had sat on the bench. As the moped drove up he squeezed on to the end of the long seat, wrapping the satchel around his immense shoulders.

xxx

Something changed within Father O'Donoghue. Slowly, the people he met everyday noticed the change. It was as if he had discovered a 'joie de vie'. There was almost a spring in his step. He stopped to nod and acknowledge people, something he had never done before and his face, which had

4

previously been buried in the recess of his hood, beamed out at all he encountered. The bishop was pleased that the collection money was coming to the mission on a regular basis. The change in Father O'Donoghue was most noticeable amongst his fellow priests, who he now engaged in conversation at every opportunity, albeit to discuss the virtuous piety of the silverback he encountered at Mopago, each time he visited.

'Unbelievable, quite unbelievable.' he announced at the table in the refectory, in between large mouthfuls of onion soup. 'If I had not seen it with my own eyes I would never have believed it!'

'And you say he is there every time you visit?' Father Devereaux eagerly inquired.

'Yes. I just rest on the bench with the takings and after a while he comes out into the clearing from the forest.' Father O'Donoghue continued, as he dipped two large chunks of bread into his soup.

'Well, it does sound rather unbelievable.' Father Devereaux conceded.

And so it continued. Father O'Donoghue and Adebayo continued their bi weekly trips on moped to pick up the collection money, stopping each time at Mopago, where the priest and the silverback spent half an hour in each others' company.

Until one day. The priest sat down as usual with his

5

rosary beads and placed the satchel containing the money on the bench next to him. After five minutes the gorilla had not appeared. He stared intently into the small copse on the edge of the forest from where the creature normally emerged. But there was nothing to see. There were no deep black pools staring back at him from the foliage as before. Then he heard the noise of a twig snapping.

'Is that you, great silverback?' He called out.

There was another cracking noise and Father O'Donoghue decided to do something he had never done before. He started to walk in between the trees and into the forest. It was much darker than he expected, as the tree canopies huddled above him.

'It is me and I have the rosary beads.'

He walked onwards, holding the beads up at his eye level and waving them in the hope of attracting the gorilla's attention. There was another noise.

'Are you there, my friend?' Said the priest, turning expectantly to his left.

The force and speed with which the knife was plunged into him meant he was taken completely unaware. But he was a strong man and he put up a fight, punching as hard as he could remember, as his old fighting instinct kicked in. His assailant flew backwards into a small bush, which immediately gave way and cushioned his fall. Father O'Donoghue looked at his side, which was now bleeding quite profusely. His cloak and cassock already had dark stains on the black material. Staggering unsteadily back towards the bench, he immediately began to feel faint. As he fell, he saw his attacker reach past him to grab the money and then disappear back into the jungle.

It was several minutes later that he came around. Kind faces of the locals lent over the elderly priest. Several local women had placed fabric on the wound to stem the blood and a small van had been requisitioned to drive him to the local hospital. He was reassured that it was just a matter of stitches on a superficial flesh wound.

Adebayo appeared in the clearing and shook his head. He had given chase, but the attacker and the money were long gone.

xxx

That evening the bishop spoke to the priests as they sat in the refectory before dinner. The normally jovial mood was sombre as the patriarch stood at the head of the table, shaking his head in disbelief.

'I am sure you will all join me in wishing Father O'Donoghue well as he recovers from his terrifying ordeal. He will eat in the ward at the hospital tonight, but assures me that he will be up and about in the next few days and will join us here then. You will also notice that Father Devereaux is also not amongst tonight. He went into Kinshasa today and received a telegram that his mother had been rushed to hospital. He has returned to Ireland and is unsure of when he will return. Now Father Williams, please will you lead us in saying grace this evening...'

xxx

Convalescing on his own in the otherwise empty ward, Father O'Donoghue cried softly to himself in the dark. He was not crying because he had been attacked. He was not crying because the money had been stolen. He was crying because he wondered if he had been a fool. An old fool. He wondered if the one thing that had given him pleasure for the first time in many years had ever really existed after all.

SwissChoc
Friday 14th February

The small shop was situated down a dingy back street in the industrial zone of Interlaken within walking distance from the Ost station, which was on the main line from Basel. If you had not known it was there you would have missed it. If you were looking carefully for it then you may have seen a very small sign attached to a post by the side of the main road bearing the slightly faded letters "Munz and Stucher - Chocolatiers" pointing down to the left.

The front window of the shop was lit by a small string of multicoloured neon lights, hidden in the gondolas of a miniature ski lift that hung from one side to the other. This framed numerous tiered platforms displaying the different varieties of chocolates in their presentation boxes; open and beckoning invitingly to potential customers. All combinations were developed, from chocolate almonds and brazils to walnut whips with strawberry swirls in between. But pride of place was taken by an intricate chocolate sculpture. Set on a pedestal in the centre of the window and measuring just over two foot high, was a small boy holding his skis smiling out at the passersby. This centrepiece was changed weekly and the local children rushed down each

Monday to see the latest creation.

Today being Friday, Christoph Munz was sat at the table in the rear workshop, working on the replacement installation for Monday morning. It was his hardest job yet, a detailed model of a carriage from the Bernese Oberland alpine railway. The brightly lit room measured about fifteen foot square and the central table was surrounded by open cupboards and shelving on all four sides. There were no external windows, just a door into the shop at the front and a door to the small kitchenette and toilet at the back of the ground floor. The shelves and cupboards stored the packaging and finished products, which were also stacked neatly on the shelving in the shop area next door.

With endless patience and a careful eye for detail, Munz set about his task with enthusiasm. Beside him on the table were two small baskets; one containing a bewildering array of tools he used for the sculpting and the other several pots of warm melted chocolate. These pots contained white, milk and dark chocolate which he used to give a sense of definition and colour to the model. Above the table, hanging low from the ceiling, a neon spotlight illuminated Munz's workspace.

Munz was a meticulous man who cycled to work each day and was particularly obsessed with his personal fitness and well-being, a not uncommon trait nowadays. It had been said that he was introverted, but he felt it was more the case that he was not given to easy conversation on small matters of no real consequence. Leaving his small chalet just before eight, he carried his carefully prepared lunch into work each morning in a small rucksack as he cycled down the alpine valley from the small hamlet of Murren, some ten kilometres away. He had repeated this routine everyday for the past three years since he and fellow countryman Stucher had embarked on their voyage as chocolatiers. He had met his compatriot at a German university where they had both studied business.

'Very impressive Christoph. Your best yet. The locals will love it!'

Munz looked up, his concentration broken by the arrival of his partner through the back entrance at nearly ten o'clock. Quiet for once, he had managed to negotiate his way through the kitchen and into the work room without the leaving his usual trail of destruction. Had he entered through the main shop door then Munz would have heard the cuckoo clock that Stucher had insisted on rigging up to alert them to the arrival of a customer. He had already been out once already to serve a tourist who had stumbled on the shop by accident and wanted a couple of standard chocolate bars. In doing so he had to negotiate his way past Stucher's desk, engulfed in stagnant piles of old flyers, invoices and letters, with just a small area cleared for current work.

'I thought we agreed you would get here early today?'

Said Munz, with mild irritation.

A sheepish Stucher looked at his watch. They had indeed agreed he would be in promptly for once when the shop opened at nine.

'Sorry. I was getting ready and lost track of the time!'

He was at least clean-shaven, with his hair groomed and wearing his best suit, Munz conceded.

Dieter Stucher was a tall man with a good covering of flesh and a mass of curly hair. His tanned, round face lit up brightly as he chatted animatedly to almost anyone he met, meaning that although not classically handsome he was considered attractive by many. Indeed, he was a very engaging man and many felt they were a good friend after a mere ten minute conversation. Unlike Munz, who spent his evenings either cycling in the valleys or at home with his wife and young child, Stucher was regularly out at the local beerkeller, listening to the oompah band and chatting to the young frauleins until the early hours. His poor time keeping and lack of organisation skills caused his partner no end of annoyance. More worrying, he often changed ingredients mid recipe, sending Munz into a state of extreme agitation.

So why, one may wonder did Munz continue the partnership? The reason was simple. It was that Dieter Stucher was the most engaging and persuasive of conversationalists. He could charm the birds from the trees, talk the hind legs of a donkey and still be a considered and supportive confidant when needed. This was an incredible gift possessed by so very few of us and least of all by the measured and uptight Munz. Whilst Munz could be relied upon to summarise the technical processes in intricate detail, it was Stucher who would charm the prospective corporate buyers over a three course meal at the local restaurant overlooking the wonderful Jungfrau.

'As it's Friday how about the beerkeller this evening?' Stucher suggested, as he had done every Friday for the last three years.

'Not tonight I'm afraid.'

The same reply, each time, which Stucher fully expected. He did not take this as a personal slight, for he knew that Munz did not socialise, whereas he himself was welcomed with open arms as an old friend in most of the local bars. Never mind, Stucher thought to himself, I will be taking the buyer from SwissChoc to lunch today.

This regular quarterly visit was the opportunity for the latest chocolate creations to be sampled by the buyer, in the hope that they would be adopted by the large producer. Although they sold a range of their own products, the majority of their income came from the chocolate balls recipe they had sold two years ago to SwissChoc, together with the rights to merchandise it worldwide. This had been the only product that had hit the big time, but based on its continued popularity SwissChoc sent a buyer on a regular basis in the hope of unearthing another gem.

Until today the buyer had been August Spiro, a fat man who chain smoked and enjoyed a business lunch even more than the greedy Stucher. Indeed, over the years they had spent many hours enjoying late lunches that flowed over into heavy drinking sessions in the local beerkeller. However, despite their camaraderie, Spiro was a shrewd buyer who refused to let his friendship cloud his business judgement. Most visits ended with a shrug or sigh and a promise that maybe next time, if the recipe was modified just slightly, an order may be placed. Except, of course, for the time when they sealed the deal on the chocolate balls. They agreed that it was the combination of Munz's clear product outline and Stucher's smooching that had produced this success.

So it was with some trepidation that Stucher now waited patiently in their workshop on that Friday morning for the first sight of Spiro's replacement. Checking his breath once more, he fidgeted around uncomfortably like a trussed turkey in the unfamiliar suit, whilst Munz coolly continued his artistry. All they knew was that Spiro was to be replaced by a buyer of similar experience.

At the same time, Frau Kurstein, who had been looking for their sign, had made her way to the outside of the shop. The quiet tap on their faded wooden door signalled their guest's arrival and Stucher, like a coiled spring, jumped up and bounded over to open it. Facing him as he opened the door, was a stout, grey haired, middle-aged woman in a conservative tweed twin piece business suit, adorned by a thick pearl necklace. She gave off a no nonsense manner, as she peered into the shop through her grey, metal framed glasses. Stucher took a step backwards; it would clearly require all his skills to charm Frau Kurstein, this would be a greater challenge than the young frauleins he was used to impressing.

For the next hour Munz took the buyer through their latest products, with Stucher looking on anxiously, trying to spot any possible weaknesses in what appeared to be a complete rebuffal of everything she was presented with. Predictably, Munz had left their most promising product until last and it was whilst tasting the peanut crème praline, that Stucher noticed a chink in Sabine Kurstein's armour. She listened patiently as Munz described the manufacturing process used and gave an outline of the recipe. Then, eating the chocolate she let out a little smile as she chewed their creation. The smile spread as Frau Kurstein closed her eyes as she enjoyed savouring the taste. Spotting his chance at this weakness in her armour, Stucher sprung into action.

'Right, now how about some lunch?'

'Well, I had not intended to spend more than the morning here' she said hesitantly, and then when Stucher made his most engaging of smiles, 'but maybe I could stay for a small snack, before I leave.'

15

For an operator such as Stucher this was the green light he needed and no more than twenty minutes later they sat on the secluded terrace of a small family run restaurant in the picturesque alpine village of Grindlewald, some five kilometres up the slopes by taxi. Service was prompt as Stucher had rung ahead on leaving the shop and the carafe of white wine, bread and local starters were already on the table when they arrived.

'No alcohol for me!' had been the strict instruction, but half an hour later Sabine Kurstein was on her second glass and laughing as she gazed into the eyes of Dieter, while he trundled out another witty anecdote. Out of her sight, he winked over at the congenial host, who ghosted subtlety over to top up the wine carafe and hot d'oeuvres. This isn't as hard as I had imagined, Stucher thought to himself and after the main course he subtlety steered the topic of conversation to securing a deal on the new product lines.

'Oh you have no worry on that score. That is the most delicious praline I have tasted in the last year. The balance of peanut, cream and chocolate is just exquisite. In fact, I have already sent them a message saying I have a new product for us to sell. It's just a case of rubber stamping it all by the administration department. It was quite wonderfully delicious.'

Now his delirium was genuine, Stucher chatted extensively and easily without even feeling he was making an effort. He was ecstatic! When at last it was time for the taxi to convey the buyer to catch the train back to the SwissChoc headquarters in Basel, they were arm in arm on the back seat. Gallantly, he waved Sabine Kurstein off at the platform of the small station after a lingering peck on her cheek. Rather tough skin Dieter thought, but it was a small price to pay. He would have kissed a week old trout if it had meant a deal on their products!

If a large man like Stucher had been able to actually jump for joy, then he would have done so all the way back to Interlaken; he was so happy. This was the break they had been waiting for. Back at the shop he passed on the exciting news to his partner, who listened patiently. After he had finished Munz calmly informed him that he felt the deal had already been done once she had tasted the praline.

'Well anyway, we have a deal!' a slightly dejected Stucher declared.

'Not until we get the paperwork' cautioned Munz.

Nevertheless, Stucher celebrated heavily that night in the beerkeller, convinced that this was their lucky break.

Friday 21st February

A week had gone by and Stucher was beginning to wonder whether they would hear from Frau Kurstein again. Had he celebrated too soon? It had all seemed so promising only a week ago; what had gone wrong, he wondered. Had he perhaps been a little forward in his entertaining of the rather introverted buyer? He tried to push these thought aside by busying himself, contacting their local buyers using phone and email.

Yawning, he put down the phone on Gunter Metalob, who owned a supermarket in the next town, after getting him to begrudgingly agree to increase his annual order from one hundred to one hundred and fifty of their novelty boxes. We're hardly going to get rich on orders like this, he thought, when he was distracted by his phone vibrating, indicating a new email. Glancing down, his full attention was drawn to the message header "SwissChoc- new contract with Munz and Stucher". He cautiously opened the email to view the contents, wishing that it would be a great deal. He read the email slowly through in detail twice in disbelief! Two million euros for exclusive rights to manufacture and distribute the peanut crème praline. They were millionaires!

He called Munz over showing him the contract offer. For the first time his colleague appeared animated. Excitedly, they both signed the accompanying contract and emailed it back to SwissChoc immediately.

'Right! Let's celebrate. Beerkeller tonight?' said Stucher. Surely Munz would finally relax and let his hair down?

'I don't think so' Munz deliberated. 'We should celebrate in style. Come to my family ski lodge tomorrow. It's free this weekend. We can ski and celebrate there.'

Stucher was shocked at this about face. He never expected that Munz would suggest any such form of bonding activity between them. He wondered how each of them would put up with the other for the weekend. Munz had made it clear there was to be no family, just the two of them. Still, this was a momentous occasion and they would soon be rich men. We will have plenty to talk about, Stucher said to himself.

There was a completely different reason why Munz had decided to arrange the trip and it was much more sinister. Following the visit from Frau Kurstein he had thought hard about their roles in the company, whilst Stucher entertained her at their expense. It was clear to him now that the success of the peanut crème praline lay solely at his door. He had invented and developed the recipe, with virtually no input from Stucher. In addition, he knew that the deal had been sealed when she tasted the chocolate, despite Dieter's protestations that it was his entertaining that had got the contract over the line. Why, he asked himself, was he getting one million, when he should rightfully be getting two? Of course, if he were the only chocolatier than he would be getting all the money.

And so a plan hatched in his mind. A plan which ended with Stucher suffering an apparently accidental death. He knew that Stucher was extremely uncoordinated and imagined he shunned any form of physical exercise. He himself had skied for years. What about getting the fat oaf on to the slopes and then arranging a slight mishap? There were lots of sheer drops near the north face of the Eiger. Nobody would be any the wiser. It would be an accident. Munz would feel guilty for taking an inexperienced skier off piste, but essentially he would be seen as blameless. Besides, Stucher had a reputation for recklessness.

Saturday 22nd February

Promptly at eight o'clock the next morning, Munz pulled up outside Stucher's small apartment in the less salubrious area of downtown Interlaken. As he had expected, the curtains were drawn, apparently indicating no sign of life. Sounding his horn, Munz settled down with the local radio on, impatiently already expecting a long wait. Instead, within a minute, Stucher bounded out in full ski gear, carrying a pair of gleaming racing skis and poles. Over his shoulder was a large rucksack, which Munz presumed must contain his clothes and toiletries.

'Lovely skis' Munz conceded, as he stacked them on the roof rack.

'Yes' Stucher sighed 'I was my area slalom champion three times in my teens. Skiing is in the family blood. My grandparents lived all their life in the foothills of the Haas mountains. I learnt there from the age of three when I holidayed with them.'

Sheisse, thought Munz, this was clearly not going to be as easy as he had first intended. Still, he found this hard to believe looking at the overweight Stucher, squeezed into the salopettes and ski jacket; hopefully this was all just bravado.

If Munz was dejected, the man in the seat next to him was ecstatic. He had not skied for nearly a year and the prospect of getting on the slopes, together with a weekend bonding with his work colleague greatly appealed to him.

As they drove out of Interlaken they passed the local garage. Perhaps he should get a new car, Stucher wondered to himself. He saw the red convertible, which he had noticed once before shining on the forecourt, priced at thirty thousand euros. That would still leave him nine hundred and seventy thousand euros. Perhaps a nice chalet in the mountains? He would be rich beyond his wildest dreams. He leaned back in the seat and imagined the times he would have in the local bars. Drinks all round on me! The most glamorous of women would be hanging on his every word each evening.

But Stucher was nothing if not a man of integrity. As he sat there, he soon began to realise that his sudden wealth would be likely to cause problems as well. People he knew would view him differently and people he did not know may want to know him. He had always been popular in his own right and he began to wonder how his social life may well be undermined now he was a millionaire. Suddenly, it appeared that his good luck could turn out to be a burden and that began to worry him.

Before he had time to think any further on the matter they had arrived at the picturesque cedar-clad ski chalet. It was nestled on the hillside, the last house on a single track that led up from the village of Wengen in the valley below, with a black run less than thirty feet from the front door. The view from the wide veranda was breathtaking, with the north face of the Eiger rising above the alpine pines at the east side of the property. There had been heavy snowfall in the night and everything looked coated in thick icing sugar. Below in the valley floor the Bernese Alpine railway trundled slowly up its single rack and pinion track, past the chalets and wood huts, rather like a child's clockwork toy. Cable cars ran parallel to the two main ski runs that finished in the village. Paragliders, like leaves, floated down on the gentle breeze, landing on the large lush green meadow beside the timber framed kindergarten, as an army of small children, skis in hand, marched to the nursery slopes. It was like the scene in a Christmas snow globe.

After unpacking, Stucher grabbed a chilled bottled beer and dropped into one of the two teak recliner chairs positioned to make the most of the view. The delicate scent of pine wafted over from the thick copses that bordered the slope. He listened. Nothing, but the sound of skis gliding over the crisp snow mixed with the bristling birdsong. What a life!, he thought.

Meanwhile, inside the shared bedroom, Munz was checking the ski runs. He had already identified the run with the most dangerous off piste area. For his plan to work, they must appear to have wandered off the recognised black run. Studying the map in detail, he saw a sharp dog leg where less than twenty yards away from the run there was a sheer two hundred foot drop to the valley below. He marked this point in pencil on the map, ready to erase it after the accident.

Five minutes later, Stucher's day dreaming was interrupted by the appearance of Munz, carrying his skis in the doorway.

'Ready for skiing?'

Stucher shot off to get his skis.

'Shall we try a red run first, before a black?' Munz asked, hoping to deflate the confidence shown earlier.

'Ok, if you want. Although, I'm happy to go straight onto a black. Last time I skied I did a black one under the Shilderhorn, about a year ago.' Stucher replied.

Ok, thought Munz. This is it. The black run it is.

'This way then,' he said as cheerily as he could under the circumstances, trudging through the thick fresh snow, gesturing for Stucher to follow him.

It took them no more than two minutes to reach the edge of the black run. First Munz positioned himself on the edge with his skis pointing down the slope, and then Stucher joined him. In convoy they sped downwards towards the end of the run, the fresh snow crunching as the skis sliced through it. At the bottom they joined the small queue for the ski lift back to the top of the run. They ended up sharing a seated lift with a middle aged French couple, intent on speaking quietly between themselves. Stucher took in the spectacular views from a lift he had not used before. Fantastic, just fantastic, he thought as the fresh alpine air filled his lungs. Meanwhile, Munz pondered on the next stage of his plan. Once they started the black run, he intended to suggest a detour off piste, approximately a third of the way down.

At the top of the run there was a small expensive restaurant and Stucher insisted on having a celebratory beer before they started their descent. Reluctantly, Munz agreed; for he was so engrossed in carrying out his plan he knew his limited capacity for small talk would be fully extinguished. As Stucher munched his way through the complimentary nuts, took large swigs of beer and trotted out some of his best anecdotes, Munz sat there as if in a daze, contemplating the task ahead, hardly touching his small espresso coffee.

'Ah well' Stucher mumbled at last, sensing Munz had become bored. 'Enough of my stories. Let's head on down.'

The start of the run had a smooth downward curve, rather like that of a helter-skelter, which served the purpose of projecting the skier down the rest of the slope at a faster rate compared to the start of most other descents in the area. Munz was surprised and begrudgingly impressed to see Stucher sweep downwards ahead of him. Each turn was executed perfectly, with the minimum of effort and the maximum of efficiency. Soon Stucher was shooting off and it was all Munz could do to maintain the distance between them. Then abruptly, Stucher pulled over to the edge of the run.

'That beer's gone straight through me.' he called over, as he stepped out of his skis and into a small copse of pines a couple of yards away. A loud belch was accompanied by the sound of a strong flow of fluid hitting crisp fresh snow. A few minutes later, he was back brushing the ice shards from his gloves and readjusting his skis. With a nod he indicated he was ready to move on.

Munz led the way as they flew down the next stage of the run. He knew exactly when his planned detour occurred. In his mind he was going over the precise details and his own escape plan. He could now see the markers ahead denoting the dog leg and he slowed to turn on to the off piste track, that was barely visibly if you were not aware of its existence.

'Slight detour, but a great view. You Ok with that?'

'No problem' Stucher shouted 'Glad to get off piste for a bit.'

Munz saw the opening, less than thirty yards away and he tried not to be tense as he led the way, knowing the gaping drop below that beckoned ahead. Then at the last minute, having generated enough speed to render his following companion unable to change his trajectory, he lurched to the right and smashed into a small wooden viewing platform. Very painful, but necessary he thought as he looked up just in time to see Stucher hurtle past him and out over the mountain edge.

There was a startled cry, like that of an animal getting

caught unexpectedly in a trap, followed by silence. Nothing. Removing his skis, Munz managed to slowly stand up. He had badly bruised his right thigh from hitting a small wooden structure and had a gash in his right palm where he had tried to fend off the impact of a tree. Cautiously, he limped to the edge and raising his ski goggles, looked out into the abyss. His first thought was to look at the valley floor directly below, expecting to see a spread-eagled mess of man and skis. There was nothing, but fresh snow. Confused, he looked further out, but still the snow was unmarked and held no clues. Instead, he moved his head to the left and saw a small ledge, about twenty foot down. Unbelievably, Stucher was climbing up a steep path from this, his skis in one hand, whilst the other held onto the branches of successive contiguous pine trees as he made his ascent. Munz was dumbstruck.

'Now that was close, and definitely NOT worth the great view!' Stucher wheezed when he finally made his way over to the edge of the drop. 'I thought I was a goner for a moment, but then I managed to steer myself in the direction of the small ledge, just as my skis left the ground.'

'Amazing, truly amazing!' was all Munz could bring himself to say.

Both slightly worse for wear after their crashes, they skied the rest of the run back to the chalet in stunned silence. There is always tomorrow, Munz thought to himself.

xxx

Later that evening after a shower they both enjoyed a large fondue prepared by Munz and several beers, brought up in the back of Stucher's rucksack; it appeared he had very few clothes in it after all. Afterwards, as they sat outside looking down into the spectacular valley lit up at night, it was Stucher who spoke first.

'Great news though Christoph? We are millionaires, who would have thought it!'

'Who indeed?' Munz replied as they clinked their beers together in celebration.

'Now this calls for a real celebration!' Stucher got up and ambled into the chalet. He returned a few minutes later with two tumblers full of an clear amber liquid.

'The finest single malt. No expense spared. I purchased it yesterday when I was in Basel celebrating our good fortune.'

'I'm not so sure.' Munz held his hand up in protest. He was not a big spirits drinker and he knew he would need a clear head to execute the plan tomorrow. Indeed, he had not expected to be staying at the chalet at all tonight.

'Come on. One won't hurt.' Stucher passed the whisky over.

Munz stared at the glass. 'No ice? What are these?'

'Ah. I thought you'd ask. Whisky stones. They've been

28

chilled so they act like ice cubes, but they don't dilute the strength like melting ice. It's the correct way to drink it, according to staff at Paul Ullrich AG, Weine and Spirtuosen.'

Munz was aware of the upmarket establishment in the nearby town- Stucher had clearly spared no expense.

'Cheers' Munz said 'Down in one.' Knocking back the whisky in one gulp.

As Munz gulped down the whisky he tasted the rich peaty flavour of the Islay single malt burning the back of his throat. The warmth filled his mouth and head in the cold evening air. This delicious sensation lasted for approximately twenty seconds and was rapidly replaced by panic as he realised that the whisky stone, which was approximately the size of a sugar cube, was stuck, lodged at the back of his throat. Gasping for breath as the stone now blocked his windpipe, Munz tried in vain to attract the attention of his colleague, who was looking over the veranda in the opposite direction.

A few minutes later when Stucher turned round, he found Munz slumped back in his seat his eyes rolled up into his head and his face a deathly white pallor. Racing to his side he cradled his partner's near lifeless body. Despite his desperate attempts at CPR to resuscitate for nearly ten minutes, there was no response. The paramedics arrived about an hour later by helicopter and soon confirmed that all signs of life were extinct.

xxx

Stucher was inconsolable and blamed himself for the tragedy. In the months after Munz's death he worked hard to set up a charitable trust in his name. He ensured that Munz's widow received the full share of his million euros from the SwissChoc contract and half of all the future profits from the business, which would continue to trade under both names. Stucher also insisted that she had full decision-making rights on the board of the company. After all, as he said, his partner would have done the same for him.

TERRORIST

NOW

J az Patel lent back against the ticket barrier and took another swig from the reusable coffee cup in her left hand. Since stopping smoking two months ago, she seemed to spend almost every waking moment either drinking coffee or chewing gum. Sugar free, of course! An hour at the gym most nights had helped her lose the pounds and she did feel better for it. She always volunteered now for any jobs involving walking to other parts of Green Park underground station where she worked. Not that anybody else volunteered. Tony, who she worked with most of the time was obese and seemed to eat Jaffa cakes non-stop, unless he was drinking from a coke can. Asif was also overweight and smoked like a trouper, while Sian couldn't even climb the stairs due to mobility issues and had to be based just on the top level of the station. It was like they'd all given up!

Today was the same as any other day. Two-tone they called it; rush hour and quiet. A bit like the Billy Connolly joke about Scotland having two seasons; Winter and June. It was rush hour, or mid evening. That was it. Almost always busy. Still it helped the hours pass and more hours meant more pay. So that was good, wasn't it? - she thought to herself.

Her thoughts were broken by a muscular man in shorts and carrying a rucksack who jogged up to the turnstile and nodded over as he held his card close to the sensor.

Just then her radio crackled into life.

'Incident on the platform! Repeat incident on the platform. Call 999 then check on progress with Fire, Police and Paramedics. We have an incident situation here. OVER'

Shit, she thought, this certainly wasn't going to be like any other day!

Suddenly crowds of passengers were running up the escalator, past Tony who shouted in vain at them to stop running, as he fell flailing after them. As she stood watching, they ran past Jaz at the turnstiles, a flock suddenly migrating with briefcases, handbags and rucksacks swirling around them.

'Run,' a young girl shouted at her, just about balancing on her heels, 'run for your life!' Then there was a massive explosion. The sound echoed along the tunnels and she saw the dense dust cloud, like a dervish, start to ascend the escalator. The sound of coughing echoed along the reverberant tunnel walls as people choked, desperately trying to cover their faces.

Jaz turned and ran for her life. Towards her came Fire Brigade staff, wearing breathing apparatus and at the entrance to the station police officers held back the crowds of onlookers, whilst ushering out the running commuters. The busker, who was there most days, was running off into the distance, guitar in hand. Only the homeless man under his faded sleeping bag needed reminding by the police to move on- reluctantly agreeing to settle down outside a coffee shop, several yards away.

Across the road from the station the news reporters were already sending footage back live to the television studios. As she ran past she heard the snatched words being transmitted.

'..large explosion at Green Park tube station. Early reports are that up to thirty people may have died in an explosion on the platform. The police have yet to confirm if this is an act of terrorism and state that all lines of investigation are currently being pursued.'

Three days earlier

Dale Smith looked in the mirror. Then he looked at the photograph next to the mirror, taken barely three years earlier. It would have been hard to spot they were the same man, he thought. The muscular, handsome guy smiling back in such a carefree way seemed a lifetime away from the haggard face framed in the mirror today. Just the one last tour, that's what he said to Janie his girlfriend before the last posting to Helmand province. Then back in three months and into "civvy street", he had promised. Some of his mates were ahead of him and had already started their own businesses in security, survival training or teaching. Janie had agreed. They had planned their future together. All that was in tatters now. The things he had seen meant the PTSD kicked in soon after he returned. Janie hung around as long as she could, but in the end he didn't blame her for getting out. His anxiety and depression became too much. She was happy now with her new guy and at least there were no kids to sort out. He had his invalidity benefits and his pension from the army.

There really was no point anymore, he thought. Nobody seemed to care, despite all the kind words. He had even met the Prince at one of the support centres. But in the end, he knew you had to face and conquer your own demons. He had given up any hope now of getting a job, despite sending off numerous applications. People couldn't be with you twenty-four seven. And slowly the frustration turned to anger. Why should he care about anybody either?

His rucksack was bulging and he had to brace himself before lifting it onto his back and practising walking with it around his cramped bedsit. Overall, he thought he should be fine carrying it around. He would spend most of the time on the train. This was a run through. He didn't want anything to go wrong. He felt resigned to this being his last chance.

xxx

She had been wearing the burka consistently for the past two months now. As she weaved her way along the Camden High Road in the drizzle, Samira Khan realised she was late for her meeting. To be honest she found that most non-Muslims were respectful of the religious and cultural reasons for her choice, which she put down to better education. However, there were still idiots who called out as she passed or directly walked in front of her, blocking her way, before issuing insults and abuse.

Today was no different. She nodded at some fellow believers coming out of the Nandos on the corner, as she walked past it on her way to catch the tube. And then, just as she was turning into the station entrance, a thug in a hoodie shouted abuse at her. Several people ran over to him as she cried out in anger, but he swore at them as he hurried off.

Half an hour later Samira was still seething when she entered the mosque and made her way to her women's meeting. Inside, when she told them what she had just experienced, the others nodded in support. They knew what she was describing all too well. She was not alone, but it was Samira who began to feel that something had to be done. She wanted to shake the general public and bring them to their senses. And she had an idea now of how she might do this.

xxx

Stephen King balanced his latte in one hand, whilst his other tightly grasped that of his eight year old son Rupert, seated next to him. This was their usual routine. Up at six thirty, showered and on the tube at Greenwich by just after seven o'clock. They repeated this each weekday so that Stephen could drop Rupert off at his prep school in Belgravia and then take the tube back to his office.

Once he had finished his drink, Stephen used his free hand to check his phone for any early office emails from the investment brokers where he worked. Rupert was already engrossed in a game on his own mobile phone. Trancelike, they changed lines at Green Park and ten minutes later were stepping into the crisp spring air of South Kensington.

Running his hands through his swept back black hair, Stephen marched Rupert round to the square and dropped him inside the entrance of the prep school. After exchanging pleasantries with a couple of other parents, he headed back to the tube, on his way to the office.

Work was becoming an issue. He was aware that Dinesh, who sat at the desk opposite him, had developed suspicions regarding Stephen's possible involvement with insider dealing. Suspicions, which as it turned out, were well founded. Stephen would have to give this problem his full attention if he was to keep his job and his liberty. As he left the tube station he was deep in thought, nearly trampling over a rough sleeper.

'Hey man!' The shout came from the sleeping bag.

He apologised and threw down a tenner.

Actually, he thought to himself, I may have come up with a solution.

xxx

The hoodie that Gaz Henderson decided to wear on his days off largely depended on his mood. Unemployed for just over a year; he had only recently gained a position at a London borough library. On days when he was not working he wore his black thrash metal numbers. Most of these had either skulls and crossbones or featureless faces with sewn up eyes and lips. A few had what could loosely be termed as pseudo Nazi memorabilia on them. Gaz did not care about the angry or fearful looks these provoked in his home turf of suburban Ruislip. This was far enough away from Clerkenwell where he worked, for him not to worry about any issues with his co workers.

Today he wore a hoodie purchased by mail order from one of his favourite bands' website. The luminous green skull starred out at the general public accompanied by an Iron Cross and a clenched fist. Hood up and head down, he pounded along the pavement as he exited Green Park station, glaring at the homeless person sheltering in the doorway. Immediately their presence put him in a bad mood. He started his quiet rant under his breath. He found there were an increasingly large number of people who seriously pissed him off at the moment, and together with immigrants and foreign workers, rough sleepers were near the top of the list. Gaz despised them. Pride of place in his hate list though, was reserved for the bankers and city types. He particularly hated the way they appeared to have the nerve to look down on him.

His new job had been a blessing, but also a curse. Gaz now had a better income than just the benefits he had before, but the downside was that the majority of the people he dealt with appeared to be what he considered to be rabid left wingers. Even worse though, were the politically correct staff that rubbed him up the wrong way during the working day. He had already had a verbal warning after a customer had complained Gaz had called him a scrounger under his breath, when he had asked if he could take an extra two books out if he claimed invalidity benefit.

He was shaken out of his thoughts as his path was accidentally blocked by a woman in a burka, about to cross the street. Wearing one of those bloody Muslim outfits so no one could see her! Bollocks to this he thought, as he shouted in her general direction, before walking off, hood down and gesturing angrily to those disgusted bystanders who tried to remonstrate with him.

Thirty minutes earlier

Dale packed his rucksack more carefully today. His trip a few days earlier had taught him that his mobility was severely hindered if the weight was too much. This was important. Mobility was all important today, he told himself. He removed a pair of combat trousers and two pairs of socks. It seemed to feel a little lighter, but he took out the rubber torch to be sure. A last look around the cramped bedroom convinced him that he had everything he needed.

The sun was out and he decided that shorts were in order, together with his old army hoodie, thick socks and a pair of well worn walking boots. He had never really been affected by the cold in all his time in the services and he could run much faster with shorts. As a final touch he had given himself a crew cut with his hair clippers last night.

It was a short walk to the tube station. He was in a positive mood, taking in the late May weather that made him realise why he had chosen to live in south west London. Walking past the parks full of joggers, footballers and dog walkers, he paced his way. It was important he was not late, as the time he had been given was very precise. They had been at pains to make that clear to him in the brief conversation on his cheap pay as you go mobile.

xxx

After making a coffee, Samira checked her Inbox for emails. She had already received one yesterday which gave her most of the information she needed. There were so many websites nowadays, that it was really helpful when someone pointed you in the right direction. So she had been thankful for the advice she had been given by one of the women at the end of the last meeting she had attended.

She had managed to collate all the information she wanted. Her mind was now made up. She realised that her actions may cause distress to some in her community, but Samira had decided that it had to be done.

Moving upstairs to her bedroom, she brushed her thick hair and applied her make-up. She looked at herself in the mirror and smiled. Today you will make people sit up and listen, she said to her reflection. They will have no choice.

Closing her laptop, Samira walked over to collect her printing from the other side of the family lounge. She had also saved the file, so she had both a hard copy and an electronic version. There was just enough space in her bright red leather shoulder bag to hold the laptop. She had made sure everything was packed in efficiently to maximise the space available.

Checking her phone, Samira realised she was running slightly late. She slipped on her white Nike Airs in the hall as she left the house. A quick walk past the local shops and she was soon entering the tube station. She held her bag close as she sat at the centre of the carriage. She had read this was the best place to sit.

xxx

Stephen King was looking anxiously at his mobile phone. He was now deciding whether or not to access the website address he had just been sent, using his work laptop. His old mate Gary who worked in IT Support at his last company had sent it to him on the promise of a round of golf in the next few weeks. It was important that he made a decision soon. Reading the email, it reminded him that the program would take about thirty minutes to fully activate. He had to leave soon to collect Rupert from his prep school.

Stephen decided to grab a last coffee from the machine in the small kitchenette, in the corner of the vast open plan office. As he walked back to his workstation he realised he had no choice. If he was to avoid serious, possibly fatal, implications for himself and his family he must deploy the programme.

Just then his phone vibrated. He looked to see he had a message from his credit card company asking him to agree a purchase on Invaders II software. On closer inspection he saw that the purchase against his card had been made by

CITYBOY. The little bugger, he thought to himself. Lately he and his wife had spend most of their time trying to keep Rupert off these bloody computer games that he seemed to have become obsessed with. On the occasions when they had confiscated his phone they found him accessing the games on their own mobiles. Racking his brain he realised that about a month back he had begrudgingly entered his credit card details into the game, following Rupert's persistent whining that he needed more credits to access the next levels that all his friends now played.

Checking his expensive watch, he realised he would miss picking up Rupert if he didn't leave now. Seeing Dinesh had conveniently vacated his desk, Stephen downloaded and opened the file on his laptop and, after selecting all connected drives, pressed execute. As the program started to run, he activated the screen saver and pushed the computer to the back corner of his desk. He had been told that the program would shut the machine down once it had completed its tasks, without leaving a trace.

xxx

Collecting his beige duffle coat from the wooden peg in the long dark cloakroom, Rupert King reached into the inner pocket and retrieved his mobile phone from amongst its soft nest of sweet wrappers. Looking around he saw lots of the boys saying goodbye as they trotted off with their coats to be met by parents or au pairs. He waved to a few friends and then wandered down the grand main staircase to a dimly lit recess of the entrance hall, where he could give the phone his undivided attention.

Keen to get further and on to the next level of Invaders II, he was also clever enough to realise that the phone held his father's credit card details, entered at Rupert's insistence some time ago. He quickly logged on and requested access to the level. In a few moments he was moving around in a different landscape. He was just scanning the terrain and working out the best move to make next, when an in-play message popped up below-

GAZBOY: 'I'm gonna do something big today!!'

He recognised the sender as somebody he had began to talk to on the game's chat room a few weeks ago. Looking around, he saw no sign of his father, who could usually be relied upon to be the last to collect his son.

CITYBOY: 'What? Level 3?'

GAZBOY: 'No man! This is the real fricking thing man!! Gonna blow them up!!'

CITYBOY: 'Really. Where?'

GAZBOY: 'On the tube man, all them bankers. Wha da' ya reckon?'

Rupert thought this was great fun; the tube must be the next level he hadn't reached yet. His thought his dad was some sort of banker. From what he saw of his work colleagues, he didn't really care for them too much. What a great idea to build this into Invaders II, he thought to himself.

CITYBOY: 'Yes. Go for it. I hate bankers!!' he replied.

GAZBOY: 'Wlico, off to do it now! Over and out!'

xxx

Gaz checked the contents of his rucksack for the third time. He had laid the grubby black and white printout on the table and was now squinting over the diagram. Getting the basic components had not been the problem, the guy in the convenience store he had visited seemed happy to sell him anything he wanted, but the diagram was severely testing his patience. He took everything out of the rucksack and then slowly tried to reassemble it again, pausing after a few minutes to switch off the thrash metal music, which for once he was finding a distraction. He even had to find his glasses, wretched things that he despised as a weakness, in order to read the small print regarding the assembly process.

Finally, content he had done the best he could, Gaz placed the finished device back into his rucksack and checked his mobile. He was beginning to get second thoughts. Gaz knew what he really needed was some form of affirmation to boost his resolve. He checked into the latest game he played,

Invaders II and entered the online chat room, deciding to place a general post and see which players picked it up.

GAZBOY: 'I'm gonna do something big today!!'

CITYBOY: 'What? Which game, Level 3?'

He recognised CITYBOY immediately. They had chatted about the game over the last few weeks. He seemed pretty sound and had totally accepted some of the extreme comments Gaz had already posted, posts which some of the other players had not replied to, presumably due to their content. Yes, Gaz was confident that CITYBOY was made of stronger stuff, like him, and wouldn't take the crap most people seemed to accept on a daily basis.

GAZBOY: 'No man! This is the real fricking thing man!! Gonna blow them up!!'

CITYBOY: 'Really. Where?'

Gaz sensed that CITYBOY was interested, hopefully he would agree the action was necessary.

GAZBOY: 'On the tube man, all them bankers. Wha da' ya reckon?'

CITYBOY: 'Yes. Go for it. I hate bankers!!' he replied.

Great! Gaz breathed a sigh of relief. It felt so much better to get agreement from another for his cause. He could hardly have discussed this with his co-workers. In truth all his friends these days where online, like CITYBOY.

GAZBOY: 'Wlico, off to do it now! Over and out!'

He logged out and switched off his phone. Throwing his

rucksack over his back and putting the mobile in the back pocket of his combat trousers, he headed outside and made his way to the nearby tube station. Despite the bright early summer sun, the hood was up and his head was down. Today he had chosen a blood red hoodie, particularly appropriate he thought.

Three minutes earlier

Dale checked his watch. He was on schedule, but the tube was now running late. It was approaching Green Park station, but he still had a ten minute walk to the address he had been given. He checked his rucksack again until he was happy he had everything he needed. As the train drew up he leapt onto the platform and raced up the escalator. Nodding at the young woman on the gate as he flashed his oyster card, he was soon out on the street and heading to his destination. Had he stopped for a minute or too, he would have heard the explosion on the platform below and heard the screams of the passengers charging up the escalator behind him.

Soon he was entering the smart reception foyer. It was a long time since he had been in such a corporate setting. Although it was spartan in comparison, he felt the setting exuded the same sense of power and authority he had felt when entering the Army headquarters on the few occasions he had been called there. The last time had been to arrange his severance when he left. His mood then had been in stark contrast to the previous time, when he had been receiving a commendation, with the top brass falling over him to get a photo opportunity.

They were running late so his interview had been put back anyway. Trying not to slump on the metal and black leather couch as he waited to be called, Dale checked through his notes.

'I am really keen to have this opportunity. I see the role of an outdoor activity instructor as a natural extension from my work in the armed forces. I have brought a rucksack full of the equipment needed for survival training...'

xxx

Samira's mobile rang and she answered the phone as they approached Green Park station. It was the interviewer from Radio London checking she had the correct directions to get to the studio. She explained that she had brought some material with her produced by the women's group at the mosque. Ten minutes maximum and she should be there, Samira told herself. This would make a real difference to take part in a balanced discussion about the role religion played in different peoples' lives.

Looking around Samira saw a man in a hoodie, rocking in an agitated state by the doors to the carriage. As he scanned the carriage he caught her eye. He looked vaguely familiar. As the train stopped he moved to front the queue to step onto the platform.

Twenty minutes later and the team at the radio station had assembled all those taking part in the debate in the green room, to run through the basic procedures. One of the crew was checking off names and passed the list of no-shows to the interviewer. She was surprised that see Samira's name was listed. Surprised and disappointed. From the selection process interviews, she had seemed somebody who talked sense and would have given a different perspective to the debate. Maybe Samira had changed her mind, she thought to herself.

xxx

Stephen King held his son's hand firmly as they sat on the down in the busy carriage. It was the very start of the rush hour and already some workers were on their way home. Others, such as cleaners, were on their way in to start their evening shifts in the now vacated office buildings. Rupert had initially been reticent in sitting next to the eastern European woman, but Stephen had insisted, forcing them into the two vacant seats. He had remembered that he needed to have it out with Rupert over the game purchase using his credit card and made a mental note to do this as soon as he had resolved the other pressing issue. Taking his mobile out of his jacket, he phoned the office.

'Ah Dinesh. Sorry mate! Can you just check I switched my laptop off? What, yeah, I'll hang on mate. Cheers!'

He had just managed to get a phone signal as the carriage had left the tunnel.

'What's that? It's already off. Thanks mate. Cheers, see you tomorrow.' Relieved, he rang off and then turned to his son.

'Now, what about using my card on your bloody computer game? Give me that phone!'

xxx

Dinesh stood behind the chair and pointed glumly at the laptop on the desk.

'It's clear inside dealing. I had my suspicions the other day and look you can see the program he has run is deleting all his files in a folder marked 'Private'. In addition, it is removing all trace from the registry, cache memory and all retrievable locations. I've stopped the program and you can see it is midway through its operations.'

His team leader leant over closer, and then looked at Dinesh and another colleague. Then leaning back he spoke.

'Right! We need to pass this onto compliance. They'll decide if this is a police matter.

xxx

Gaz fidgeted with his phone. No bloody signal, he thought to himself as the carriage rocked through the long tunnel. Just my luck! Looking around he could see the carriage was packed, mainly with tourists. Not many city types like the bankers he had targeted, he had to admit to himself. Few seemed to be wearing their uniform of expensive tailored suits, most instead in jeans and causal coats. The only space he could find was just beside the doors and he already been pushed twice when the train stopped in the last station, both times swearing into the face of the culprit.

Now the train was approaching Green Park station. Nervously, he quickly checked the inside of his rucksack. Everything was in place. Gaz had used instructions from the internet to set his mobile phone so it could activate the detonator. As the doors open, he flicked to the app on the phone. It was taking a long time to load and he could sense agitation in the people behind him, who were keen to disembark the carriage. For maximum impact it had to happen just as they all stepped down onto the platform. Finally the app loaded, presenting him with a large green virtual button. He was aware of a man shouting at him from the queue behind. Gaz turned around.

xxx

Rupert looked up in despair as Stephen grabbed the phone.

'What's this? You're on a bloody chat room?' Stephen stared in disbelief.

As Rupert turned away sulkily, Stephen checked the phone messages. Much as he tried to stop it, he could feel his blood pressure rising as he scanned down the conversation. There was CITYBOY, the name Rupert had used to purchase on the credit card. Scrolling up he could see that the conversation was just between Rupert and somebody called GAZBOY.

'Who's this GAZBOY?' he demanded.

'No idea dad, just an online friend. Never met him.'

Oh no, my credit card! Stephen thought, as he began to feel a vein start to throb on the right of his forehead. But then he could see the messages were more sinister. Was this GAZBOY really intending to blow up the tube? What was this fascination with bankers?

He had lost track of time as the train jolted to a stop at Green Park station. Roughly, Stephen grabbed Rupert's arm and joined the queue to get off. Even though the doors had opened, nobody had moved. Stephen craned his head past two women ahead of him.

'Bloody well get on with it!' he shouted.

A man in a blood red hoodie turned around. Then, looking in his direction and pointing straight at Stephen, he shouted.

'A BANKER!'

The man's hand moved on his mobile phone. Then it all went black.

A kind of loving

His was the last caravan in the row. Far away from the centre of things. Away from prying eyes; just how he liked it. It was rather run down compared to the newer versions and he didn't have a garden plot- just a yard for the bins and the whirligig clothes line; the latter currently struggling under the weight of his last wash.

He had lived here for nearly five years now. You were meant to vacate them for two months of the year, but he was employed as site manager, so he could stay all year round.

There was a loud knock on the kitchen door. That would be Ken.

'I've brought Barbie. Put the kettle on!' The northern voice boomed through the spring air.

'Bring her through. I won't be a minute.' He tidied the rubbish off the coffee table and plumped up the sofa cushions.

Moving through to the bedroom, he sat down next to Juliet. It was a small room, with most space taken up by the queen size double bed, draped in a bright pink duvet cover. The two cheap wardrobes that clung to the thin walls were packed. Quickly he changed her clothes and re-arranged her hair using her hairbrush. He just needed to add a little more red lipstick, just how he liked it.

When he entered the cosy lounge, Ken was already seated on the old patterned sofa that had seen better days, with Barbie next to him. He placed Juliet in an armchair and then sat down in the other himself. Three times a week on average they met up as a foursome. He had always been single and had no kids. Ken had been divorced a long time ago. Then one day over a pint in the pub down the road, Ken told him all about his new girlfriend.

'You too,' he said, 'even a dull lad like you could bag a beauty!'

'Put the match on and I'll grab us some cans.' Said Ken, entering the kitchenette.

He found this rather disrespectful to the girls, but Ken insisted, telling him that they could "chat between themselves while we watch the footy."

Nobody else shared their charade. It was their unspoken secret. His mother, who died recently, had sensed that something had changed.

'Have you got a girlfriend son? Really, at your age?' Yes he bloody well had, he had thought. And so he showed her the photograph. He can still picture her now, bending over with a smile. Then those beady eyes squinting and that furrowed brow. 'She's bloody plastic!! '

He hadn't meant to hit her. For many years she had been his life. She had died very recently. But he couldn't have her saying that about his Juliet.

xxx

About a month later, the four of them were sitting in his lounge "taking tea", as Ken liked to call it. Best china cups; strong builder's brew for Barbie and weaker for Juliet, neatly laid out on the small occasional table. His mother's funeral had gone ahead in the last few days, after the coroner had signed the death off as natural causes, once he explained about the unexpected fall in the night. Ken was moaning about how the campsite was filling up in the last couple of days, when he stopped mid-sentence, jumped out of his chair and flung the front door open.

'Bugger off, you little bastards!'

Two boys in their early teens were riding outside the caravan on bikes, laughing and making hand gestures.

'Eh mister, you've got a cracking young girlfriend.' One shouted, whilst the other boy giggled uncontrollably.

Ken lurched at them. The whole scene looked ridiculous as he stood at the open caravan door. The boys gestured again and, avoiding Ken's angry lunge, cycled off.

It was all he could do to drag Ken back inside. When Ken finally sat into the lounge his face was bright red. A "high colour" his mother would have called it.

'Little bastards were looking through the window.' Ken spluttered.

He looked to where Ken had pointed. They could only

56

have seen the backs of the girls; just saw the slim figures and the blonde hair, he reassured himself. Fortunately, there was a football match on the TV that took their minds of the incident.

When Ken finally got up to leave over an hour later he had calmed down sufficiently to reflect a little.

'I think we need to be a little more careful about the girls' profile. Maybe we should be a little more secretive in our movements with them outside the caravans.'

He nodded. He knew Ken was right. If he looked at it objectively, it did seem crazy for two grown men, but he put these thoughts to the back of his head.

xxx

It was late on a bright summer morning that he heard a loud rap on the door. Peering through the net curtain he saw a young policeman standing next to the boys.

'I am sorry to bother you sir, but we have received a report that you are holding a young lady here against her will.' The boys sniggered in a particularly knowing way, which made him feel even more uncomfortable.

'Really, I'm not sure where that report came from?' he said, stepping back. 'Come in and have a look around.' Once the policeman was over the threshold he glared at the boys and slammed the door firmly in their faces.

'I can assure you officer, that nobody, least of all a woman, is being held here against their will.'

With that he nipped into the bedroom, while the policeman searched the kitchen and lounge. He knew now what he had to do, and in a split second he grabbed his nail scissors and punctured the inflated body that lay on the bed. Then in the same movement he compressed it to remove most of the air, placing it in the bottom draw of his small bedside table.

After spending approximately half an hour checking all the possible hiding places, including two wardrobes that held a large amount of the gentleman's elderly mother's clothes, the policeman left satisfied. He was slightly taken aback by the raunchy nature of the lingerie which the old lady appeared to have a penchant for, but on reflection he decided to keep these thoughts to himself.

xxx

Later that evening he sat down in the lounge armed with a cup of tea and a packet of custard cream biscuits and switched on the TV. He had not yet had a chance to let Ken know about the police visit. To be honest, he was quite shaken by the whole experience. Channel hopping, he was unable to settle down and put it out of his mind.

After an hour or so he realised he missed the company.

Why be alone when he did not need to be? It made no sense. Entering the bedroom, with the curtains now drawn to protect from prying eyes, he took the plaster he had just found in the bathroom and placed it over the rip in the fabric. Hopefully one would do the trick. After all, it would just look like a plaster, which anyone could be wearing. Slowly he pressed down on the foot pump and the lifeless body began to inflate...

The Signal

I caught her eye as she stood behind the counter, serving tea and scones at the village fete. It was mid-April and although the sun was hot, the air was still cool inside the marquee. I had seen her in the village before of course; they had moved into the old house attached to the pub. Her husband was an accountant in the city and occasionally I saw him leaving in his new expensive car when I looked out of my bedroom window. They didn't have any children and, according to my mother, she didn't have a job.

'Not sure what she does all day, housework I suppose?' She had said over breakfast one morning.

My dad grunted something about being a kept woman, before he looked at his watch and wandered through to the Post Office and shop he ran from our front room. It seemed destined to close as they had in some of the neighbouring villages, but he said we had enough trade to get by at the moment.

And so I plucked up the courage and moved over to the table she stood behind, resplendent in a bright red caftan, her blonde hair held up by some intricate bird's nest of hair clips.

'One cream tea please?'

'Well thank you kind sir. That'll be three pounds.'

It seemed a bit steep to be honest, but I handed over a fiver. As she gave me back the change her hand lingered just a moment too long on mine, caressing rather than touching it. I felt the blood rush to my cheeks.

'Oh you're blushing. Sorry!' She said. And then quietly, in my ear as she leant forwards. 'What's your name?'

'Richard, Richard Worgans.' I managed to get out, feeling my shirt beginning to stick, as rivers of sweat ran down my back.

'Well Richard Worgans, I hope I see plenty more of you in the future around the village.'

I picked up the tea and scone and nodded as I turned away. She winked back.

And so it began. In the following few weeks I seemed to bump into her all over the village. After the Evensong church service, when I was serving in the Post Office, when my family had Sunday lunch in the village pub, while I was at the bus stop and so on. Each time she smiled and nodded knowingly and then, when nobody else was watching, winked. It was a signal.

xxx

Walking back across the fields from having tea at a friend's house one day, I saw her standing watching me from the track that ran up to the windmill at the top of the hill.

61

Under her arm was a wicker basket and as I approached I saw she had been picking blackberries that were growing abundantly from bushes at the edge of a small strip of woodland. It was a common spot for foraging at this time of year.

'Hello Richard Worgans!!' She called over. 'How are you this fine day?'

'Hi, Mrs Jones.'

'No, really. Call me Cynthia.'

'Hi, Cynthia'

'Now tell me Richard Worgans, just how old are you?' She said as she wagged her finger in my face.

'Eighteen.' I said confidently. And then a little reluctantly. 'Well, in a month or so.'

Leading me by the hand, she opened the back gate to her garden and walked me down the path and in through the patio doors, through the lounge and up into the master bedroom. She told me her husband did not get back until five thirty at the earliest, later if he went for a pint in the pub. It was four o'clock. She drew the curtains, closed the bedroom door and undressed.

And so it began. We began to meet regularly as lovers. My college course was only a twenty minute bus ride into the outskirts of Reading. And of course, there were days when I had gaps in my timetable; afternoons off and late starts.

We had some close shaves. I spent half an hour in the

wardrobe one morning, when the next door neighbour came round to persuade her to help out at the church jumble sale. The bloody woman more or less asked for a cup of tea and piece of cake, even though I could hear Cynthia trying to escort her off the premises.   And then there was the time when her husband came home early with a migraine and nearly interrupted us in the actual act. I climbed out of the guest bedroom window carrying my shoes and most of my clothes. I had to wait behind their garage until the local farmer had passed, before I sidled up to the bus stop as if nothing had happened. Which it very much had, obviously! I am not sure my appearance from the undergrowth fooled the vicar's wife who was waiting there.

Now, lying beside each other in the bed sharing a cigarette, she said to me.

'We need a signal.'

'We've got a signal. You wink at me when we see each other. That's our signal.'

'No!' She said shaking her head. 'Not that, silly. A signal, for when it's okay for this.'

'Oh, Okay. Trumpet fanfare?'

'No, don't be stupid.' She slapped me playfully. 'I know. I'll hang a pair of Eric's green gardening gloves on the washing line if the coast is clear. Then if anyone is already here, or planning to arrive, you'll know because the gardening gloves won't be there.'

'Perfect, green gardening gloves it is.'

So we agreed.

xxx

Soon my college course broke up for the summer and our liaisons increased rapidly. Unless I was asked to work in the shop or was out with friends, I was free pretty much all the time, and with my younger sisters to worry about, my parents took no interest in my movements. Before every meeting I checked to see if the green gloves were hanging there, rather like traffic lights signalling the all clear.

I became accustomed to the surroundings of their master bedroom. The William Morris wallpaper, "The strawberry thief" I believe, and matching curtains. The king size bed, with its pock marked brass bedstead, and crisp, fresh cotton sheets and eiderdown. The polished oak- veneer furniture. And I remember spending a lot of time looking at a damp patch above the window.

One day, when I was serving in the shop, she bloused in and winked as she waited in the queue, cradling a Daily Mail and packet of extra strong mints. The few elderly customers present appeared oblivious to our ongoing liaisons. After patiently waiting while Mr Sharma emptied his pockets as he searched for enough small change to pay the postage on a parcel, she finally reached the counter. Handing me the five

64

pound note, she passed a slip of paper. Later, on my break I read it in my bedroom.

"ERIC IS AWAY TONIGHT IN LONDON. COME AND STAY OVER. PLEASE! C xx"

My brain whirled into overdrive as I planned the cover story to feed my parents. Not sure if staying at a friend's would hold water if they probed at all, I came upon what with hindsight seems a ridiculous plan, that I was camping that evening with college friends over in Reading. I hurriedly set about searching for my old tent from the dilapidated wooden shed at the bottom of our cottage garden. Waving goodbye to my sisters, I waited patiently for the hourly bus, with the tent and a sleeping bag under my arm. When it stopped in the next village, I dismounted and stashed the camping gear in a bush behind a small electricity sub-station on the outskirts, before taking a footpath which led pass the back of Cynthia's house.

As I bounded down the garden path, she opened the back door to great me. Armed with a large glass of red herself, she handed me a bottle of cider, similar to the type I presume she had seen me drinking in the local pub.

'Steak for us tonight,' she informed me, as she brushed her lips against my cheek, wet from sweat.

We ate in the beautiful dining room with low beams and

an enormous inglenook, seated opposite each other at the oak table. Mushroom soup, then steak and chips and finally profiteroles, which I wolfed down. When I congratulated her on her cooking, she threw her head back and laughed. 'It's all from Waitrose silly!'

'You know,' she said, 'you're so lucky being young', as she sipped her third glass of wine.

'But you were young once!'

'Yes, but I never made the most of it. That's my big regret. I never realised it was that good until it had gone. You are having the time of your life now Richard Worgans and don't you forget it!' She wagged her finger mockingly at me. 'Just remember once you settle down with someone it becomes so much more complicated.'

It didn't seem like that to me, as I helped her load the dishwasher and pour another drink. In fact, domestic bliss seemed strangely inviting. Stupidly, I told her so.

'Oh, you may think that. Just wait until you have to consider somebody else all the time. It's much easier to be free and single. You can remain contented just doing what you like and not have to tread on eggshells to please the other person.'

'Is Mr Jones really that difficult?' I asked, somewhat naively.

'Oh I don't mean Eric!!' She almost shouted back at me.

She sat there in silence, staring moodily out through the

window at nothingness of the now pitch black back garden, whilst I stared embarrassingly at my plate. Then just as quickly, she jumped out of the trance.

'Leave the dirty plates we can do them in the morning. Let's go to bed!'

Next morning, when Cynthia was in the bathroom, I lay there and turned to examine the side table. I picked up Eric's bedtime reading and his partially completed crossword book. There was a black and white photograph of a couple smiling at the camera, with a young boy standing shyly in front of them. There was a small tumbler for his water and a pill box. The final item puzzled me until I realised it was the container for his false teeth. As she returned I sheepishly turned away, embarrassed by the intimacy of it all. Then, instinctively, I blurted out.

'I love you!'

'Don't say that!' She said turning away. 'Please don't say that!'

'Why not?' I stood up. 'I want people to know. I want to shout it from the window!' I moved theatrically over, pretending to open the curtains with a flourish.

'No, it's not funny. Really, it's not. Please don't say it again Richard!'

Admonished, I slumped back on to the bed, lying there sulkily, with the wind taken out of my sales. She lit a cigarette and smoked it in silence beside me. I stared at the damp patch, while all the time she looked away. When we dressed we did so quickly, without looking at each other. I knew the spell was broken.

xxx

Sure enough, I did not hear from Cynthia again and I noticed that she began to keep a low profile around the village over the next few weeks. On the few occasions I did see her, she avoided my attempt at any eye contact and instead turned to talk intensely to her husband. I checked the washing line, but the green gardening gloves never re-appeared.

And then, several months later, I was at the bus stop with a few minutes to spare and decided to wander back up the path for old times' sake. Of course I couldn't resist checking on the garden. And there, on the line, were the green gardening gloves. I felt a lump in my throat. Obviously, they are just being cleaned I tried to convince myself.

In a daze I walked back to get my bus. Looking into the distance I could make out the red top deck, as it turned past the large horse chestnut tree bordering the vicarage wall. Much closer the front door of Cynthia's house caught my eye. I focussed hard and saw the son of the local farmer, a year younger than me emerging. He looked furtively around, before scuttling home up the footpath opposite.

The General

He looked up from behind his paper, just a small almost imperceptible movement as he scanned the room. Although having clearly seen better times, it was still a rather upmarket independent hotel on the English Riviera, not one of those ghastly chains he thought to himself. The room itself displayed the air of slightly decaying Edwardian grandeur and possessed ten tables, all of which had already been laid for dinner. Running along one side was a long oak sideboard, dressed with a starched white tablecloth, on which a number of serving dishes were mounted.

In one corner a pair of young honeymooners stared into each others' eyes over half finished plates and half empty glasses, completely oblivious to the fellow diners. A waiter approached, momentarily breaking their trance to inquire if the food was to standard and then scuttling away to the side of the dining room to collect and deliver more freshly prepared dishes. Nothing to interest him here, he thought.

As his eyes moved to the centre of the imposing room he saw an attractive older woman, dressed in county casual tweeds, struggling with her mobile phone. Ah, this was more like it! The table was laid for one, always a good sign, and the freshly filled bread basket indicated she had yet to eat. In fact, she had not been there when he last scanned the room twenty minutes ago, before he had read the report on the recent test match. It wasn't the same now Cook has retired, he said to himself. Still they were making a good fist of it against the "Kiwis", but they were hardly in England's league. And what had happened to the mighty "Windies" these days?

After a few minutes careful observation he assured himself that the woman was travelling alone. There seemed no sign whatsoever of a companion. He folded his paper and put it down as he straightened his tie and smoothed back his thinning grey hair. Checking his brown brogues, he polished them surreptitiously on the back of his trousers. He was halfway out of his seat and with the paper already wedged under his arm, when a booming American voice stopped him mid action.

'Excuse me mam, surely you're not eating alone! Care if I join you?'

He watched as the man strode over and plonked himself at the table, while the woman looked up from her phone. Bugger! The General sat back down. A few minutes earlier and he would have been seated next to her. Instead he spent the next hour drinking a second coffee and checking his shares, while the American relayed his life story in between stuffing apparently vast quantities of food into his overworked mouth.

The only other diners were a middle aged couple. An

elegant slim man who had clearly aged well and had made the best of himself in an unobtrusive way sat opposite a tired looking woman in a rather dowdy dress. She appeared to be nervously fiddling with a wedding ring, whilst the man chatted to her.

On reflection, the General decided the best option would be to dine frugally alone. He had just started tucking into his plain omelette and salad, when he was aware of the presence of the honeymooners at his shoulder.

'Sorry to bother you,' the man asked meekly, 'but we understand the famous singer Tony Zorro is resident at the hotel?'

He stared up at them vacantly. 'Sorry, I've no idea what you are on about!'

He carried on eating as they walked away crestfallen and left the dining room. It was when he had finished and sat back in his chair to allow the food to digest that the idea came to him.

After leaving as small a tip as deemed acceptable, he marched into the bar and settled himself on a stool, indicating his usual Whisky Mac to Pierre the bartender. The bar was deserted apart from the older woman and the American, who had followed him in and now sat huddled together, chatting enthusiastically at a small table by the window. The General sighed wistfully, as he couldn't help noticing that the woman appeared captivated by the American, roaring with laughter each time he reeled out an anecdote.

Ten minutes later he had quietly outlined the full plan in confidence to Pierre, who the General had already identified as an accomplice by his greedy manner and suspicious eyes. He had been correct in his choice, for Pierre clapped enthusiastically as he outlined the execution and sealed their pact with a second drink on the house.

xxx

The next day, an hour before lunchtime, the General sat in the drawing room reading the paper, his worn brown leather armchair pointing through the open doors into the cavernous entrance hall. He had carefully arranged the position so that he could see everyone entering before they reached the reception desk in the foyer. It was a light room, with a varied selection of potted plants and walls lined with watercolours of the local area, providing a peaceful ambience. Other guests passing would assume he was giving the paper his undivided attention. The smell of cooking, drifting in from the kitchen, did nothing to suppress his longing for a good lunch.

It was just after the large grandfather clock beside the piano had struck a quarter past the hour that his wait was rewarded with the appearance of the honeymooners, entering the hall, hand in hand. Sensing the moment, as they shook the light rain off their coats, he quickly sprang into action.

'Can I apologise for my rudeness last night? Allow me to introduce myself. General Bagshott.' He was standing by their side in the hall, head bowed slightly.

The couple looked suspiciously at each other and then, having clearly come to a mutual agreement, both lent forwards and shook the general's hand.

'Yes, most unfortunate I must say. And of course you were right!' He added.

'Right?' Inquired the woman.

'Yes, about the singer staying here. Allow me to explain.'

'Really?' Said, the man keenly.

'Yes, Are you eating?' The General inquired.

'Er yes' the man said. 'Would you care to join us?' The words were out of his mouth before he realised what he had said.

'Well, yes, thank you very much.' The General indicated to the dining room with his outstretched arm and was seated with the A la Carte menu in his hand within a minute.

Of course, the couple realised that they would be expected to foot the bill in return for the information the General would supply over diner. It was, in essence, an unspoken contract. In return, the General, ordered the most expensive starter, main course and dessert, a fact that did not go unmissed by the couple.

'And so you see,' said the General, as he sliced his

enormous steak, 'you were quite right. My sources in the hotel informed me that he is staying in an exclusive suite on one of the top floors.'

'Tony Zorro! Well, he is my wife's favourite entertainer,' said the man, as his wife nodded vigorously. 'And it would make her honeymoon, if we could meet him.'

'Yes,' his wife added, 'I have got all his records and I've seen him in concert several times.'

'Ah.' The General sucked through his teeth as he finished the morsel of steak in his mouth. 'That could be difficult you know. I understand he is somewhat of a recluse.' After all, he had decided, it was important to give the impression that gaining a meeting would not be an easy task.

'Really?' Said the man. 'He doesn't come across like that on TV, does he Carole?' The girl shook her head vigorously in agreement.

'No, he seems so relaxed and natural. I read he always signs autographs.' She added confidently.

'Er well, when I say recluse, I mean when he is staying in hotels he likes to keep himself to himself.' Said the General, backtracking fast.

He changed the subject to general chit chat as they completed the main course. It was as they were finishing their crème caramel that the General broached the subject again.

'Anyway', he continued, 'my contact at the hotel will

keep me updated. I will see if I can arrange a meeting for you.'

'That's fantastic, isn't it darling?' said the woman.

'How about we meet for dinner this evening and then we can visit his suite afterwards?' The General said sagely.

The man nodded, his attention distracted as he looked at the substantial bill and placed a card beside it on the small silver platter the waiter had subtly left on the edge of the table. Ten minutes later, and with the promise of a further update soon, the General bade them good afternoon and retired to his small room at the back of the hotel for a rest.

He was careful to make sure they were unaware he had one of the cheapest rooms, which overlooked a small cluttered yard, where the smoke from the staff on cigarette breaks mixed with the burnt fat from the kitchen extractor fan. Hanging his dark blazer and slacks back in the small cupboard, the General noticed that his few shirts were beginning to wear thin on the collar. An injection of cash was sorely needed to his finances.

The hotel had a strict no smoking policy and he had briefly considered taking a walk in the grounds now the recent drizzle had subsided, but eventually decided to risk having a cigarette, whilst leaning out of the window in his room.

xxx

That evening before dinner the General nipped into the bar for a quick aperitif. On the house of course, now that they were co-conspirators! However, there had been a slight hitch in sourcing some of the clothes needed, so regretfully Pierre informed him that the invitation would have to be delayed until tomorrow afternoon instead.

So, with a slightly revised plan, the General met the couple in the dining room at just before eight o'clock. It was clear that the woman, Carole, had gone to some considerable lengths in preparation for the meeting. Not that he generally noticed these things, but she had changed her hair and make-up and was wearing much more glamorous clothes than the previous evening.

As before, the General chose three courses, including the premium steak dish. As he devoured the food he made positive noises of acknowledgement as the couple relayed their afternoon adventures, firstly to a nearby castle and museum and then on to the neighbouring small town. Carole spent a long time outlining the merits of a small tea room that the General made a mental to avoid. Boring as he found their mundane adventures he played the interested listener well. It was when they were served deserts, that he broke the news regarding the planned meeting.

'Sadly, he is unwell!' He said bluntly. 'He is not even

having a meal from room service tonight.'

'Oh, no!' Carole looked genuinely upset as she dropped her spoon. It was clear that she had indeed gone to a lot of effort.

'I am sure it will be fine by tomorrow afternoon', he said. And then, adding a morsel of comfort, 'he knows you want to meet him and he's looking forward to it.'

He felt slightly ashamed at embellishing the whole fiasco with such a brazen lie, but it seemed to settle the couple and a further half hour was spent with more extended small talk over coffee. Politely nodding at regular intervals, he listened to details of their engagement, the proposal at their workplace, the wedding near to her family home in Hampshire and their honeymoon. Once again, the couple insisted on paying- the General was indeed their guest. An offer he duly accepted, after only minor protestations.

He mounted the stairs to his room with the satisfied feeling of having dined well. Later, as he lay on the bed he mused over how long this could be strung out for. Delicious though the food was he was finding the couple's company far less enthralling than his usual elderly companions.

xxx

The next morning it was raining and the General decided to read the broadsheet paper in the conservatory. Normally

77

he avoided the room at all costs as he found it too hot and very often it had the added side effect of being plagued by swarms of small insects that appeared to inhabit the large number of indoor houseplants. However, today he had made an exception as the overnight rain had brought cooler weather.

He had already heard from Pierre that John, the dishwasher in the kitchen, had been identified as the member of staff who most resembled Tony Zorro from the photos on the internet and they had now managed to source some retro vintage clothing similar to the star's stage wardrobe. It was all set for after lunch in one of the vacant suites. They had decided that one hundred and fifty pounds would be a reasonable price for a signed photo, which they would split three ways between them. All in all, three free meals and some petty cash seemed a good reward for a simple ruse, he thought to himself.

Having checked on England's progress in the Test Match, the General was just assessing the potential value of a particularly fine print hanging on the wall opposite, when he became aware of the arrival of a marked police car on the expansive hotel drive. The conservatory provided him with a particularly good vantage point to view the proceedings that were unfolding outside. Two uniformed officers stepped out of the car and made for the hotel entrance across the gravel. Remembering some of his activities in the previous hotel, which he had had to leave so abruptly, he slipped further into the armchair and retreated behind his newspaper.

There was the sound of a commotion coming from the front of the hotel and raised voices. A few minutes later the police returned, accompanied by the honeymooners, who they promptly bundled unceremoniously onto the back seat of the police car. Looking up from behind the paper, he saw that the man looked suitably crestfallen, whilst the wife appeared to be berating him. However, the General was sure that the man had given him a knowing wink when he caught him looking in their general direction. Bloody cheek, he thought to himself!

When the car had disappeared up the drive he put down his paper and made his way around to the main reception desk. The Hotel Manager, who was still there, immediately beckoned the General over. He appeared to be in a somewhat agitated state.

'I see the police were here?' The General inquired as casually as possible.

'Yes, I called them.' The manager said quietly. He looking tight lipped. 'Credit Card fraud. Terrible business! They used a stolen card to pay at the hotel!'

The General was genuinely shocked. 'Oh, dear!'

'Yes. I was alerted today on our payment system. And you of course dined with them.' The manager paused for effect, leaving the sentence hanging in the air. 'However, I informed the police that you were just a casual acquaintance and not an accomplice. It was pure chance that you shared several meals with them.'

'Yes, thank you.' The General nodded. 'Pure chance of course. I'd never met them before they spoke to me here yesterday.' He added quickly.

'But under the circumstances I am sure you would like to pay your part of the bill just to make it clear.'

'Err yes, just to make it clear.' The General repeated.

'So let me see. I believe you had the premium sirloin steak both times, together with starters and deserts and half the champagne, as I believe the wife did not drink.'

'Quite' mumbled the General.

'Altogether that comes to, well rather a lot actually, two hundred and twenty seven pounds and sixty four pence.

Reaching into his blazer to retrieve his wallet, the General winced.

Just at that moment the single older lady he had seen yesterday descended the main staircase into the foyer on the arm of the American. He noticed that they were deep in conversation, with the woman repeatedly throwing head back in laughter. Leaving through the main entrance, they both got into the back of a chauffeur-driven Rolls Royce.

Following the General's gaze, the Hotel Manager remarked.

'Ms Cotterell is a famous writer and a millionaire. She has

taken quite a fancy to Mr Seibel, the American who is staying here. I am not sure what he does, but she seems infatuated.'

The General settled his share of the bill and was about to make his way to the bar to break the news to Pierre, when he became aware of a new arrival queuing at the reception desk, signaled by her delicate perfume. Straightening his tie, he slowly turned around to introduce himself...

Enclosure

A zoo located in South East England, circa 1900

L ewis Johnson stayed towards the back of the crowd that had surged forward towards the large wrought iron gates, for this was a moment long anticipated since the news of the ill-fated trip to central Africa had been relayed back to England by telegram. Staff and local people had grouped inside and outside the zoo respectively, together with a swarm of press photographers and reporters, who jostled for the best viewpoints. The park was closed to the general public and the return had been cloaked in secrecy, as befitted such a bittersweet expedition.

The zoo's Director of Animals, Godfrey Simmons, and his young wife had set off in search of the fabled 'gorrilaze' or 'dancing silverback', as it was called by the local peoples. Rarely seen, even in its natural habitat in the Congo rainforests, it was said to be the primate most closely resembling humans. Privately, Lewis had seen this as no more than a publicity stunt to generate public interest in the zoo that had, quite frankly, fallen on hard times. Combined with his dislike for Simmons' lack of animal knowledge and condescending attitude, he consequently found it hard even now to find much sympathy for the man's gruesome death.

Details were scant, but essentially it appeared that Simmons had overplayed his hand in getting close to the beast and had been savagely killed in front of his wife. The hue and cry that now ensued at the zoo entrance was caused by the transportation of the caged beast in the third carriage of the entourage. It was to be the zoo's star attraction, just as Simmons had intended.

The zoo owner stepped forward, helping Eleanor Simmons climb down from the front carriage. It was she, rather than Simmons himself, who had expert zoological knowledge. The crowd cheered as she dismounted. A date had been set for the funeral for her husband in the local town church, but this was no grieving widow that now stood before them.

'May I present,' said the zoo owner clearing his throat with a flourish 'our new Director of animals!'

'On, no!' Eleanor replied. 'I am afraid I cannot take on that role. I will be fully occupied as the keeper of our newest primate, the gorillaze.'

And with that she pulled back the curtains to reveal the only example of the animal in captivity outside Africa. The crowd gasped in awe, but as the assembled array of box cameras flashed, Lewis could see that the creature was well-hidden with just an arm protruding from a pile of straw. The entourage quickly moved to the sanctuary of the small wooden barn, which was to serve as the primate's sleeping quarters.

xxx

The zoo opened to the public the next day, but the enclosure of the new arrival was cordoned off from view. In his role as a ranger, Lewis did not specialise with one particular animal, but instead undertook personal tours for the more wealthy visitors, providing detailed information about each of the animals they visited. The creature was, of course, the only talking point. Indeed, many of his customers had tried to tempt him with large sums of money, to allow them a preview of what lay behind the hastily erected facade.

Once the zoo had emptied its last visitors for the day Lewis made his own way to the edge of the large billboards attached to the enclosure netting, which were emblazoned in pictures proclaiming the new attraction, but were installed primarily to block its content from prying eyes.

'Mr Johnson!' a female voice called urgently across to him and he could see Mrs Simmons waving him over to where she stood about fifty yards away.

'Mrs Simmons, my condolences. Your husband was a good man. We had our differences, but no man deserves to die that way'. He said, as he walked towards her.

'It's broken my heart!' She sighed.

Brushing away her tears, she walked over to his side and

continued 'But I must throw myself into my work now. You are just in time. We are releasing the new animal into his permanent enclosure.'

With this she signalled to the primate keeper who was already inside the fencing. A surly bull of a man in his late fifties, he barely nodded an acknowledgement before opening the gate and nimbly retreating through the outer exit. The beast wandered slowly into its new surroundings, before appearing to take a good look around the enclosure. Almost fully upright, from a distance it closely resembled the outline of a man with a loping gait. Suddenly it become aware of the onlookers and bounded away to the farthest corner from public view, beside the small barn.

From his brief initial glance, Lewis could see that the animal had a full covering of hair over most of its body, except its face. What struck him as strange were its limbs, which closely resembled those of a human. The arms hung differently to other primates he viewed on a daily basis. Lewis had spent the last five years observing these animals at close quarters on his tours. Studying the movement and behaviour of the animal before him now, it was clearly unlike any he had seen before. Then, just as he was leaving something the animal was holding glistened and caught his eye.

Lewis moved closer to the fence and peered through the wire mesh netting. From his vantage point he was fairly sure it was a piece of glass. The more he looked it appeared that the animal was holding some kind of lens. In fact, thought Lewis, the object looked very similar to the pince-nez that Simmons used to wear when he was reading. Catching his eye, the creature briefly stared back and then quickly bounded into its indoor sleeping area, hidden away from view.

xxx

Later, back in his cramped room at the keeper's lodge, Lewis could not sleep. In the black silence his thoughts circled repeatedly around in his head. He was becoming increasingly convinced that the animal was more human than ape. Could it be that Simmons, whose body had never been recovered, was acting as the star attraction? After all, only his wife had witnessed his death. In addition, the animal was his height and body shape, with its limbs in the same proportion. When he thought about it, he also remembered that Simmons had swung his legs in the same way. Furthermore, why had his wife insisted on being the animal's keeper, rather than taking up the more prestigious Animal Director role on offer?

In that instant, Lewis formed a plan. Acting it out, he jumped out of bed and dressed quickly into his uniform of khaki shorts and shirt. He crept outside to the gun store, taking out one of the rifles and enough tranquiliser to just stun a man in case he needed it. It was dawn now as he strode towards the enclosure and the animal was nowhere to be seen. The silence was broken only by the soles of his hard boots on the dirt path, amid the first throes of bird song. Unlocking the gate he marched over to the bedding area in the half-light, calling out to Simmons as he did so.

xxx

The small stone church in the village overlooking the zoo was full. The sun shone through the large stained glass windows and the knave was decked in flowers; the air filled with their perfume. People were openly weeping as the coffin was borne past the crowded pews on the shoulders of the keepers. After a few minutes, the zoo owner stood up to address the congregation.

'We will never know what possessed Lewis to enter the enclosure of this wild beast armed with only enough tranquiliser to stun a man, rather than a wild animal...'

Guilt

Peter and Judith were justifiably proud of their semi-detached house in the leafy side street of an Outer London suburb. They had lovingly improved it from the 1930s original, which had been built as part of a pre-second world war housing scheme. Unlike many of the others houses in the road they had tried to maintain all the original features, sourcing double glazing that resembled the metal frames and choosing retro radiators and doors.

Peter frowned now as he looked out of the freshly cleaned front room window at the street, congested with parking on the grass verges. He shook his head at the front gardens; nearly all had been replaced with paving, packed with cars like commercial garage forecourts. He understood this reduced congestion, but why not have just one car and use the garage for what it was meant for, instead of a DIY playroom full of noisy tools that interrupted most of the sunny afternoons he spent relaxing in his back garden.

With abundant, well-pruned trees and shrubs, theirs was the only frontage in the street that had any sign of wildlife; apart that is from the wilderness that surrounded the dilapidated home opposite. Flora sprouted everywhere, rather like the facial hair of the recluse who lived there. Most of the cars appeared to belong to the offspring their neighbours couldn't seem to shake off. Whereas, their two girls had moved on to university and careers making lives of their own.

He sighed. One shouldn't be too smug, Peter reflected. A responsible lifestyle, based on moderation in most things, had meant that they had paid off the mortgage and their final salary pensions more than covered their living expenses and holidays, allowing them to support the girls on the rare occasions they needed it. He was aware that Judith had just come downstairs into the room.

'Ready?'

'Yes' he said. He could smell the aroma of fresh coffee wafting from the kitchen.

'Now are you sure? There's still time to change our minds. They'll understand and nobody will think any less of us.'

'No' said Peter. 'We agreed. I think it is an excellent idea from the Rotary Club. If we can sponsor Remi and his brother by giving money to help the family smallholding back in Romania, that is the best kind of charity in my opinion. It should give them a step up that will last for future years. We both agreed we can afford this donation.'

The doorbell rang. Through the lounge net curtains, Judith could see two men patiently standing outside the front door.

'Here they are now', she said, turning and making her way

through to the entrance hall.

xxx

An hour later a large bald man, who had introduced himself as Remi, was sweating profusely and leaning forward on the sofa next to Judith in the front living room. On the small coffee table was a collection of cups, and an empty plate which had held biscuits and cakes, all eagerly consumed by the visitors. Another large man and Peter occupied the pair of comfy armchairs in matching fabric to the sofa.

Against the opposite wall was a small upright piano, faces smiling out from the photographs carefully arranged on top of it. Mahler played in the background at suitably low volume and there was a subtle aroma of citrus from an M and S candle burning on the mantelpiece.

They had all already spent a good half an hour looking at photographs of the extended family, that lived in a rural hamlet nestled in the Carpathians, as Remi had passed his phone between them. Tired faces looked into the camera, while carrying out a range of menial manual and agricultural tasks. It was clearly a tough life. To be honest, Peter had seen enough. He didn't want to say anything, but he was getting bored and had already tried to attract Judith's attention on several occasions. No luck! Still at least the men had turned down the offer of more tea or coffee.

'The main problem is need for fresh water. They need

pipeline from further down the street to get running water for animals .' said Remi in broken English, with a heavy eastern European accent.

'And for the houses as well.' added the second man.

'Oh no!' said Judith, 'You mean that they don't have fresh running water in their homes for cooking and washing? '

'Is Okay,' said Remi 'they are used to it. The children carry a large bucket of water back from the well every morning. That is usually enough for all cooking and clothes. Then they get more for the washing later. They share outside toilet between houses.'

'No' interrupted Judith 'It is not Okay is it Peter?' Peter nodded blankly at the mention of his name. He was hoping this was going to finish before he missed the golf highlights on BBC 2.

'Peter and I want to give you a cheque. We understand some of the other members of the Rotary Club have already helped you out. Peter, give them the cheque.' She gestured to Peter. 'Is five hundred pounds enough?'

'Thank you. Thank you very much.' Remi replied.

Pocketing the cheque, he rose and the two men said their thanks, leaving shortly afterwards.

'Great, that all seemed to go very well!' Peter exclaimed, as he hurriedly filled the dishwasher and settled back down in the lounge. After a frustrating few minutes, he located the TV remote under a sofa cushion. The golf was on before

Judith had re-entered the room.

xxx

Walking back to their car, parked a few roads away, the two men were in deep conversation.

'I'm not sure' said Mick in a south London drawl, 'basically we are conning them. They think we are eastern Europeans who need a charity payment. It's just a con.'

'Look, didn't they say they wanted to help people less fortunate than themselves?' Andy replied, dragging on his recently lit roll up. 'Did you see how happy they looked when I explained how their money would help all the people in poverty back in Romania?'

'Exactly, but it won't.'

'I know, but they think it will. People like them have so much spare money and are so comfortably off that they feel guilty about those less well off than themselves.' Andy leant back and blew a few smoke rings into the cold evening air.

Mick tried to follow this logic. 'Ok, but the fact is the money is still not going to where they expected.'

'But they think it is. And that's the whole point. They will feel they have done their bit. After all much of the money given to charity goes to into the admin and pays staff wages. So it's a win-win. We get money and they feel less guilty!'

'A win - win' Mick reflected. 'Yes I suppose you're right.'

xxx

I am really pleased that we did that today. It gives me a little warm glow inside thinking that our money has helped others less fortunate,' said Peter, lying on his side of the king-size double bed and resting the open book on his lap. His side light was still on and he had just finished a chapter of the latest thriller he was reading.

'Yes dear' Judith mumbled from under the sheets, her light already out. She was tired now, but used to Peter droning on while she was trying to get to sleep.

Yes, thought Peter as he switched his bedside light off and nestled under his side of the duvet, maybe I'll look at that catalogue tomorrow for some new leather car seats. Just at that moment his mobile vibrated on the bedside table beside him. At first he didn't recognise the number, but then he realised it was the chair of the Rotary Club. This was late! What did Rodney want at this time of night? Frowning, he pressed accept and took the call.

The Panic Room

'Don't forget to read the reset procedure notes...'
With a last dismissive nod, Karen ejected the engineer from
the house. She had certainly had all she could take of his
patronising droning on. He had done a decent job
completing the panic room, but now she was anxious to
inspect it herself. One the few faults she would admit to, was
a necessity to understand every detail of any new project she
was involved with, whether at work or home, and this was no
different. Denis, her partner, admired this in her. Karen
smiled as she remembered how Den would always say, 'I
thought I was tough, but you've got more balls than me!'

Recently they had been forced to replace the five foot side
fence with a much higher version, running down the full
length of the boundary of their extensive residence. They
both appreciated their privacy and had become annoyed after
repeatedly catching the next door neighbour leering through,
under the pretence of fixing his property. The south facing
garden was their pride and joy, and they spent as much time
as possible there, either gardening or sunbathing.

However, the couple had become conscious of the
increased spate of burglaries in the area. Politics of envy
meant that the imposing property stood out, together with
their high performance cars parked on the enclosed courtyard

driveway. Neighbours at the other end of the village had recently woken up to find intruders in their house and had a knife held to their throat until all the valuables had been pocketed by the thieves. The plan was for the panic room to provide a secure area for them and their valuables while they waited for the police if there was a break-in.

The room was located off the main hall, approached by a disguised panel under the stairs. It was relatively small, about twelve feet square, with no windows or noticeable entry or exit opportunities once the door was closed. On one wall was a very large smart TV which was linked to show continuous live footage from each of the nine security cameras the engineer had installed around the inside and outside of the property. Next to this was a wall-mounted landline phone.

On the back of the door was a complex lock which activated a nine point secure locking system and a further two cross bolts. The hinges were also concealed and the whole door and all the accompanying fitments were manufactured from high tensile strength steel. It was now time for a practice run, Karen thought, as she closed the door from the inside. It glided back into place with a very solid, very reassuring, very expensive-sounding thud. She pressed the close button and the electric motors whirred as the locks moved securely into place. Satisfied, Karen stood back and scanned the whole room. The CCTV monitors blazed relaying all activity from outside onto the big screen. Perfect. She felt totally safe.

Currently the room was bare and unfurnished. Den and Karen had selected some expensive reclining chairs, in the lazy boy style that were to be delivered next week, together with a solid oak bookcase and coffee table. They were also awaiting the arrival of a range of inspirational prints purchased off the internet to cover the walls. Might as well be waiting for the police in comfort, they had said to themselves. Unable to sit, instead she stretched out, doing a few yoga exercises on the polished maple floor, whilst admiring the room.

xxx

It was a few minutes later, whilst in the downward dog position, that Karen first noticed a problem with the CCTV screens. Initially she assumed that the cameras had lost their connection. Soon it became clear that the TV screen itself had lost power. The overhead light was still burning brightly, but had a built-in power storage facility. Expecting this to be the same for the electric entry door, she was shocked to find that there was no response. Picking up the landline phone she found that this was also dead.

After spending some time checking, it was clear the electricity supply to the room was cut off. At least she had her mobile with a reasonable charge in her pocket. This registered no signal, presumably as a result of the metal walls of the room. Karen began to worry. It was early summer and the temperature in the room was getting hotter with no air conditioning units operating. However, Den was due back tomorrow evening and Karen estimated she should survive a further thirty-six hours without food and drink. If the necessary, she could always strip down to the underwear she was wearing, purchased by Den for her last birthday. At the time they had laughed over the skimpy lingerie; now it served the minimum of purposes as the heat intensified. She had tried shouting, but realised pretty quickly that the room was completely sound-proofed.

Reflecting on her predicament, she wished they had not been quite so hasty in dismissing their gardener about a month ago. The guy had been fairly lazy and the final straw was when both Karen and Den found him relaxing in a secluded area of the garden, drinking a beer with his feet up on their expensive garden furniture; their attention initially having been drawn by the slight wafting of a weed smell through the kitchen window. "Taking the piss!" Den had called it and Karen agreed. His nonchalance when accepting the dismissal with a shrug, illustrated how little the job appeared to mean to him. Now she realised that had he still been working, he would have been due in today and perhaps he may have searched for her at some point to check on his instructions. Although, she reflected, his lack of diligence meant that this was less than likely anyway.

Not normally one to lose her composure easily, Karen was now beginning to panic. The 'Fit-bit' she always wore on her arm was flashing wildly like never before and was making a buzzing noise. She saw her blood pressure, usually low, had rocketed to sky high. Ripping the device off her arm, she angrily stamped hard on the small screen, smashing it to pieces. To make it worse, she had developed a nagging thirst and regretted that the time they had wasted deciding on the correct water cooler meant it had not yet arrived.

Looking around the room there appeared no possible means of escape. The only break in the four walls was the door. With no windows they were polished completely smooth and flat, as was the ceiling- apart from the air conditioning vents which were beyond her outstretched reach. Indeed, the white featureless colour scheme that had so appealed to them with its fresh clean feel, now felt imposing like a prison cell.

Then Karen looked closely at the TV screen, surely it must be wired in somehow- was there a conduit hidden somewhere? The screen itself was set into the wall at head height. Slowly she moved around its perimeter, tapping the surface of the wall with her keys. Each time she heard the solid thud. Still she preserved. Moving an inch at a time this was a slow, painstaking process. Then, just below the centre of the bottom of the screen there was a slightly lighter sound, with a hint of it being hollow.

Using her keys she picked patiently at the plaster. It was very slow work. Although she had small hands, the house key was not the ideal implement for the purpose and kept dropping onto the floor. Nearly an hour later, the plaster was removed enough to show the wires for the video feed and the mains connections. Picking away frantically now, Karen loosened the wires and slowly managed to pull at them. With one final, hard pull, they broke away, coming free in her hand. As they came out she could see a very small star-like source of light. Putting her eye to the hole and looking through it, as if it were a telescope, she saw the outline of a small stone bench, flanked either side by flowering shrubs. This was the location usually chosen by the gardener for his regular breaks. The irony was not lost on her.

This was a massive setback, but Karen was nothing if not resourceful. Her tough upbringing and her fight against prejudice meant she had developed a very hard exterior. A protective coating that deflected all the barbs and comments had allowed her to pursue a very successful career, without caring what others thought. True, there had been staff not up to scratch; and they had been summarily dismissed. In essence, they were in the wrong job. Of course, she did help those who wanted to improve, but her business relied on having staff that could deliver and she could not carry makeweights.

Only the last week she had put a consultant on competency. He left the meeting in tears and later that day his wife had marched into reception, demanding to see Karen. After a fairly acrimonious exchange in her office, the woman turned on her heels, shouting 'You hard, callous bitch!' over her shoulder as she marched out passed the shocked admin staff.

But this was just the most recent case. On deeper reflection, she knew there had been many similar ones. Karen did not dwell on them at the time or since. Okay, some had apparently attempted or considered attempting suicide, but nobody had died. Most were extremely disgruntled employees who moved on, developed other careers and in the end consigned their memories of her to a box that they had no intention of ever opening again.

xxx

But not all did. Gerry Smith loved his daughter Shelley dearly. She was the apple of his eye. She had always been a daddy's girl. It was he and not his wife who took her swimming and to Brownies when she was younger. It was he who picked her up from nightclubs in her teens and twenties in the early hours, to avoid her having to use taxis or walk. In fact, you could say he was overprotective of her. Nobody was prouder on the day she graduated with an upper second in Business from Manchester University. Then she landed the dream job and started her career as a recruitment consultant. At first her parents were pleased to hear how supportive her new boss was. The promotion that came at the end of her first year and the large Christmas bonus were more than they had ever experienced themselves.

Then Shelley became more withdrawn. She socialised less. She started ringing in sick to work. Concerned Gerry had a heart to heart with her. Amazed at what she told him he found it hard to believe that someone could undermine a colleague so much.

'I'm not the first' she told him 'Her PA has an expression she uses. "On the bus" means she wants to get rid of you dad. It's me next. I know it!'

'Well, just get another job, love.'

It's not as simple as that dad. She is very influential. She

101

sits on loads of committees and boards. Sure she'll give me a reference. But nobody will employ me for a decent job. They'll want to know why she doesn't want me anymore.'

'It can't be that bad, love'

'It is dad! When I came back to work after my last sickness I had a meeting with her. She said she was putting me on targets and competency.'

'What about the unions?'

'Don't be silly dad. They will support you, but you career is finished as soon as you use them. You're seen as toxic and nobody else will touch you.'

He shook his head. How could this have happened? It had all seemed so promising less than a year ago. Now Shelley seemed immersed in depression. He suggested a change of career, but knew that she had her mind set on recruitment.

A week later, they got a phone call from her neighbour in the upmarket block of flats where she lived. Water had been running into the flat below and when they gained access to the flat she was found slumped in an overrunning bath, an empty bottle of sleeping pills on the window ledge. Fortunately, the quick thinking neighbour had called the paramedics and they managed to get her into hospital, where they had pumped her stomach.

After that they had moved her back in with them. She never returned to work and he and his wife were on round the clock suicide watch. He had taken time off from his business. His partner understood. They had run the security company since they left school. Initially it had been just replacement locks and installing strengthened doors. Then they had moved into more sophisticated security systems with movement sensors and linked cameras. The latest developments were panic rooms for more wealthy clients.

He couldn't believe it when he saw the name on the order. Immediately, he decided he would do this installation. He always did an excellent job and his quality this time was the same as usual. It was the timing that was crucial. He knew that the local council were developing the nearby bypass. There had been a note in the local newspaper that he spotted stating the days the work would be taking place. There was no mention, of course, of any power cut but that did not matter. He scheduled the job to be done during this time.

After that it was all really quite simple. All he had to do was temporarily disconnect the mains electricity, once he checked Karen had entered the panic room. He did this using his laptop as he waited around the corner in the van. After all, he set the system up so it would not be unexpected for him to have access to all the footage from the cameras. Once she entered the panic room and shut the door, he cut the cable at the end of the garden. In his company overalls all any locals would see was a security expert accessing the wiring. Then after five minutes he reconnected it. Nobody would be any the wiser. If she had listened she would have heard him explain about the reset procedure and how it would get the system unlocked after a power shortage. He knew she would not listen. He knew that the system would therefore not operate, until somebody else reset it. Even if her partner, who he had seen driving off loudly in a flashy sports car as he arrived, returned and looked for her, they would just find a locked door to the panic room.

Of course, they may try to contact the company, wondering where Karen was and why she could not open the door to the panic room. But his partner was on holiday for three weeks in the Maldives. And he was thinking of taking the next few days off himself.

<u>Ken</u>

en Murray sighed as he looked at the empty glass and half
finished crossword on the table in front of him. He had
Konly meant to nip in for a swift pint at the end of the week.

Now, four pints and a whisky chaser later he was feeling
decidedly worse for wear. The pub was beginning to empty
of early evening drinkers anyway; his usual cue to leave. He
managed to stand up, and after several attempts, disentangle
his battered jacket from the back of the chair and make his
way to the toilets, acknowledging the barman with an
unsteady wave.

It seemed like an age that he was slumped against the
urinal, first waiting for the small trickle to start and then for it
to finally stop. Time was he could pee through an open
window without relying on gravity. Fortunately, there was no
young buck in the urinal next to him firing powerfully at the
target like a shooting gallery at the fair. A brief splatter of
water on his hands and he turned to go, catching himself in
the mirror. Jesus, what had become of him, he thought? The
luxuriant curly brown hair had long gone and the piercing
blue eyes were now hidden in the recesses of his skull, behind
high prescription bifocals. Then there was his gut. Talking
of which, he needed to seek out some food.

Stumbling into the local chip shop a few doors along, he

managed to quell the rising tide of beer approaching his throat, and after placing his order, sat by the window. It was then that he became aware that somebody, Frances Leworthy from his year seven maths class to be precise, was staring in his direction from the seats opposite.

'Helloo' he spluttered, drunkenly, saliva frothing around his mouth. Quickly he wiped it away.

'Excuse me, who do we know you?' a woman, who he took to be her mother, demanded.

'I am her Matffs teacchherr'

'At St Joseph's? Really! Is this correct, Frances?'

The girl nodded vigorously. He was indeed her maths teacher. In fact, he was her favourite teacher.

'Oh Yessh, First class honours from Cambridge. Thirty years in the saddle.'

Her order ready, the horrified Mrs Leworthy urgently ushered Frances out to their car.

A few minutes later, clutching his cod and chips, Ken opened the condensation-draped door and stumbled out after them. The cold evening air burnt his eyes and his face immediately flushed for warmth. No longer able to put off the inevitable, Ken promptly turned and vomited into a bin outside the entrance.

Turning back, he was just in time to see Mrs Leeworthy glide past in her Mercedes, Frances sat in the back grinning broadly in his direction.

'Oh God!' he thought.

xxx

Lurching away from the shop he managed to negotiate the fifty yards to his flat, just. Inside he collapsed, prostrate on the sofa, switching the television on. Surrounding him, hanging like un-ironed tobacco leaves, where half dry items of clothing. He made a mental note that most of his underwear was so old it had become 'crutchless' and he needed to replace it. On the coffee table was an array of discarded dirty plates and out of date newspapers. Scattered on top of the half completed crosswords, were a collection of pens. One of the perks of the job, he always said. Free stationery. That and the holidays.

After a few seconds switching between channels, he settled on a programme where a panel of middle aged women were discussing the relative merits of breast reduction surgery. Ken's interest was roused by the particularly attractive woman who was chairing the debate and seemed to possess breasts that needed no reduction at all in his opinion. Then he remembered his fish and chips. Just in time. They were nearly cold. He dowsed them in salt and vinegar and wolfed them down, together with a can of strong lager that had been residing at that back of his fridge for longer than he cared to remember.

It was some time later that he was awoken from his drunken slumber by a light, but persistent drumming on the flat door.

'Ken, can you turn the TV down please? I'm trying to get some sleep. Sorry.' A quiet voice asked as nicely as possible. It was Gail Halfpenny from the flat above.

'Course, sorry Gail' he slurred back embarrassingly, for he found Gail particularly attractive.

He checked his watch. Bloody hell, it was nearly one o'clock! He managed to clean his teeth, change for bed and get a glass of water before he was once again sound asleep.

A few hours later, needing his regular pee, he glanced to the side of him. Good God! Gail was lying naked beside him in the bed, looking at him longingly through her thick black eyelashes, her mouth forming a full pout. Quickly he checked the top drawer of his bedside table and gulped down the Viagra tablet he kept there with a little water. Much better, he thought. Turning back he got another shock. It wasn't Gail at all now, but the old biddy he often saw on the bus into town. She smiled at him, coquettishly opening her mouth to reveal a tongue peeping through the hole in one of the mints he often saw her sucking on the front row. And to think he had given his seat up for her on several occasions! Startled he jumped out of bed, banging his head on the door and waking up fully in the process.

After an hour the pain subsided. He had checked and he

now had a bright red stigmata on the front peak of his bald head. Great! When he finally dozed off at just after three o'clock, he had consoled himself with the fact that there was no school for a few days.

xxx

On Monday, with his wound partially disguised by some concealer applied by Gail, Ken cycled the mile and a half to school. He had been embarrassed by the procedure, but Gail had been very understanding. During the five minutes that she was attending to him, he tried to keep putting the flashbacks from his dream the other night firmly to the back of his mind.

He kept his head down as he free wheeled into through the school gates and around to the staff bike rack on his faithful old racer. After dismounting, he entered the school through the side door of the main building, heading for the staff room.

'Ken, the Head wants to see you. He just came in looking for you.' Jenny Jones, a good friend of his called across to him from the far side of the room. She was sensible, mid forties with a slight lisp and taught Food Tech. They put the world to rights over their sandwiches on the days when they managed to grab a lunch break. However, he wished she could have been a little more subtle. Several of the more trendy young teachers smirked as they saw Ken visibly flinch at her words.

Bollocks! Ken thought. That bloody parent! He straightened his tie and cleaned his glasses, a nervous action of his, before marching head down to the Head's office.

Through the glass he saw Frances Leworthy and her mother being addressed by the Headteacher, confirming his worst fears. He knocked.

'Ah, Ken, come in. You know Frances and this is Mrs Leworthy.'

Mrs Leworthy gave him a withering glance and a brief nod.

'Yes, hello. We met the other evening. Can I just say..'

'Sorry Ken,' the Head interjected 'but we're a bit short of time and as you can see we have the press here.'

Oh no, he thought, not the press, spotting a middle aged man standing in the background with an expensive looking camera hanging around his neck.

'Anyway' the Head continued 'I suspect you are wondering what this is all about?'

Of course he knew.

'Well..' Ken ventured.

'To get to the point,' the Head interrupted him, 'as you know all students in year seven get a chance to enter the National Maths Olympics. '

Ken knew this. He didn't really agree with it, but the

Headteacher and the Head of Maths pushed for this, supported by the more demanding parents.

'Anyway, Frances here has come top in the whole of the county. That is why we have the local press here today for a photo and the story. And she wanted you to be in the photograph.'

'Yes, Mr Murray' the young female reporter added 'she has already told us how inspirational you have been to the whole class in lessons.'

Ken starred at the group meekly, unable to quite take it all in. To be fair, Frances was an excellent student, who was a pleasure to teach. However, he had not made any attempt to coach her and whilst he considered himself a good and conscientious teacher, he was not sure how much glory he could claim for her success.

'Yes.' Frances interjected 'I told them how you taught us fun ways to remember algebra. You know you said multiplying out the brackets- the way to remember it is the term outside the bracket is a friend, and they have to talk to each of the friends inside the bracket individually so you multiply out the terms?'

Yes, he did remember that. One of his more inspired moments, he reflected.

About ten minutes later it was all over and Ken left to register his class. As he turned and said his goodbyes, Frances gave him another broad smile. He headed off down the corridor, with head held high and a spring in his step.

Fatal Infraction

Downtown Bus Station 5.30pm

His eyes had to refocus as he entered the large room. It was dusk outside and now the neon lights blazed above the waiting queues. Accessing the bus station in central San Francisco had been fairly straightforward. Looking around he saw people of all shapes and sizes; tired families dragging their kids and as many possessions they could carry on their way to visit relatives, laughing college students with their rucksacks on vacation and loners seated or standing quietly their own, avoiding eye contact. One thing drew them all together in this drab and humid room- limited budget.

The space seemed overfull of people and he wondered how many would be travelling on his route. To get to the automated ticket machine at the far wall he had to negotiate a river of sticky liquid flowing from its source in a large tub of hummus, discarded by its owners who had boarded an earlier coach. Cautiously, he made his way further inside past the other passengers.

He had not travelled by the Greyhound bus before and it took a while for him to navigate around the screens on the interactive terminal. Choosing the contactless option, he purchased a single to Santa Cruz and looked around for a

seat. The bus did not leave for another hour and he decided
to check his phone for mail and then browse the internet. A
large poster on the wall opposite proclaimed free wi-fi and
displayed the security code. Nodding, he sat next to an old
couple who were holding hands and blocking out the world
from their own private silence. Was this what people mean
by love, he wondered?

He would have to remember to stay on the bus at San
Jose, being careful not to confuse it with Santa Cruz and get
off early. Sometimes the similar words could confuse him
and he made a mental note to ask the driver to remind him of
the correct stop.

Becoming bored of his phone and increasingly hot in the
stale air of the enclosed room, he moved to just inside the
entrance doors, seeking out what limited cool breeze he could
find. From here he could scan the waiting passengers more
clearly. The old couple were now moving to board at a bus
outside and more people were joining the ticket machine
queues. A weary cleaning employee, sweating in the company
uniform, wandered aimlessly around the whole station area,
emptying the bins and picking up rubbish. Through the
doors he could see where several homeless people had tried
to bed down under the scattered old cardboard outside the
main entrance.

He was now aware of a presence by his shoulder and
turning he saw a young guy who promptly offered him a cold

114

drink. It was stifling in the room now and he was beginning to feel a little unsteady. Thanking him, he gulped it down without a second thought. His attention was drawn to a commotion at the front of one queue. An elderly man was trying unsuccessfully to pay using contactless on his mobile phone, drawing groans of agitation from those waiting patiently until now in the queue behind him.

'Hey man, get on with it. Use your card!!' said a bronzed "college jock" type, impatiently leaning over the man's shoulder.

'OK, ok, I just worry it's not so secure' the man sighed.

He could see a woman looking away, slightly embarrassed, further back in the line. Her bone structure was exquisite and her skin tone was neither dark, nor light, but almost perfectly in-between. In repose her face seemed to display that symmetry between the position of the eyes, nose and mouth. He knew about this; the golden ratio, so revered by the ancient Greeks as a measure of beauty. When she caught him looking she smiled, and in that instant he was smitten. Looking away, he now realised his biggest fear. He was devoid of easy charm and wit and, rather like a room without an echo, he provided no quick comebacks to keep the conversation going. And yet, although he was unsure why he felt this way, he knew he had to talk to her.

A news stand next to him showed glossy front cover photographs, but as he studied them he could see none had the attractiveness of the face of woman in the queue. Turning back he now saw a man stroking her hair and paying her close attention; he could not believe it! She was moving her head back and forth, and opened her eyes and mouth wide, clearly she was enjoying it. Perhaps she had been approachable after all. Dejected, he realised that on the balance of probabilities his chance had most likely gone.

He had been warned that security was high in these places, and sure enough, he saw a large woman in a black outfit and a holstered gun, enter the room from a side office. People in authority always caused him some confusion and he immediately went on the defensive, apprehensive that he may need to be ready to answer any questions. However, her immediate focus was clearly the homeless group outside the entrance doorway, which had grown in number as early evening darkness had begun to set in. He watched as she slowly moved them away from their position, chosen for maximum proximity for begging money from bus customers, and around the side of the building to a more concealed area. Clearly not happy about this they moved reluctantly, mainly due to a combination of the woman's pleasant attitude and the threat of the unconcealed weapon.

She now strode back into the room and was carrying out spot checks on ID for the waiting passengers. To be fair, this did not seem to focus on any particular race, colour or gender, but appeared on the face of it to be completely random. After patiently waiting for the old couple to recognise that the she was addressing them and then locate their ID cards, she was checking their details.

Now she stood in front of him and held out her hand. Cautiously, he handed over his document.

'So' she said 'You work at the university?'

'Yes, I am in the computer science department. A researcher'

'Thanks, everything is in order. Have a safe journey.' She said handing back his ID card and moving on.

He had momentarily forgotten about the woman, but he was relieved to see that she was now alone, sitting in the same spot reading the magazine. Trying to draw as little attention to himself as possible he skirted around the edge of the room, intending to finally drop casually into the seat that was now empty next to her. In all this took a good minute, although it seemed far longer and he could sense a tense throbbing in his forehead. There seemed so much to take in and frankly he was beginning to become overwhelmed by the anticipation of the impending meeting.

'Is this seat taken?' he said as she looked up. 'Or can I join you?'

'Of course. I'm Steph, pleased to meet you.' she said, moving slightly to the side and smiling again to reveal those perfect white teeth.

'I'm Mike, good to meet you too.' he said, settling down

and holding out a hand. She did not respond, instead keeping her hand resting in her lap, on top of the magazine. He glanced and saw this was one of those he had spotted earlier. Preparing to start a conversation on the main article, he was surprised when she started talking.

'Are you travelling far?' she asked.

At this moment he could just hear the call for the Santa Cruz bus over the speaker system in the background. This was now a big dilemma. Should he get up and go, or stay to chat with her and miss his bus? He had never been able to make such quick decisions, always needing time to process all the information provided and evaluate the best option.

'Yes, my bus is not due for a while. Where are you heading?'

'Portland.'

'Same for me! Maybe we can hang out when we arrive there?'

He knew there would be consequences for lying, but he knew this route was not going south as he had originally intended.

'I don't really understand?' Steph replied. She was shaking her head vigorously, 'Why would we want to do that?'

'Well, I think you're pretty cute and I'd like to get to know you better', replied Mike, surprising himself by coming straight to the point.

'I don't really understand, why would we want to do that?' Steph repeated, staring blankly forwards, appearing to focus on an object on the far side of the waiting room.

Oh dear, Mike thought, this is not going to plan, when she let out a small gasp similar to a tyre deflating.

'Executing shutdown process.' a metallic voice emitted from her lips as her eyes closed and her head lowered.

'No!' cried Mike, 'I don't believe it. It can't be. What a fool I have been! No wonder you have such beautiful features.' His arms began to hang heavily at his sides. Dejected and confused, he felt the energy drain from his own body.

Local University Computer Science Laboratory 6.30pm

Back at the laboratory Mike and Steph were slumped lifelessly in office chairs, looking like they were sleeping off a heavy night out. The room was brightly lit and a range of computer screens displayed traces of the sensor data. Printouts of the voice generation transcripts lay on the main table in front of Gary and Taylor. Running his finger over several of the sheets, Gary spoke first.

'Hey, Steph performed well, locating the machine, waiting in the queue and buying the ticket. Then successfully moving around the area and taking a seat. It would appear all the program features tested worked correctly in a real-life situation.' Gary said. 'After I went in and recalibrated her eyes, she managed to focus on Mike and respond to all the prompts given. The data suggest all visual, auditory and motion sensors worked correctly. The servo motors in the head and body meant mobility tests were all passed for negotiating obstacles. Gestures for the head in talking and responses were deemed almost lifelike. Same for Mike?'

'Err, not entirely', Taylor was shaking her head. 'Initially all was fine. He purchased the correct ticket and his movements were all correct. It just looks like something happened after Gus topped up his servo motor fluid, checked his CPU fan and tightened his auditory receiver. Initially, after that, he did still behave as expected when Amy played the authority figure checking his ID. His data shows the correct degree of anxiety and anticipation for such a situation and the algorithm executed correctly for the input data from his sensors.'

'Ok, so that's good, right?'

'Well, yes, but..' Taylor voiced trailed off and she was now looking at the data on the screen more intently. 'For a start, he didn't execute the next stage and did not go to the bus when it was called, even though the data shows he clearly picked up the message and deciphered it correctly for program execution. It appears that the execution of the sequence to go to the bus was stopped- sorry I mean overridden. The only other activity at this time was a dialogue with Steph.'

'Seems strange.' said Gary 'No programs were overruled when he interacted with Amy as she checked his ID documents?'

'No, the recorded speech data shows he developed an unexpected attraction to Steph, but that does not make any sense. Nothing in the program allows for this. I can't understand why, but he seems to have overridden the logical outputs that should have been generated, in an attempt to stay and generate a relationship beyond the interaction these androids are programmed for. It looks like there was an infraction of the rules within his cognitive algorithm.'

'Oh dear, that's pretty fatal. Looks like we'll have to scrap Mike and develop another android brain,' sighed Gary.

'True, but that's not the most worrying part. It's clear that he actually identified her as an android- something way beyond his scope and totally unexplained. In fact, he seemed to think that he was human!' gasped Taylor.

Pet Shop Superstar

Returning to my home town to visit my elderly father, I had an hour to spare whilst his toenails were brought back to some form of normality by the NHS chiropodist. As I passed the medieval town hall, one of the oldest in England, I remembered that a friend's family owned an independent pet shop in between the Turkish restaurant and the opticians in the next row of shops. It was still there, with a new luminous sign and a window full of treats to temp in the prospective customer. Upon entering and asking how Mr Stevenson was, the middle aged lady on the till at the front of the shop informed me that he had retired and Ted had now taken up the reigns. Better still, he was in the back room and had just finished sorting out the recent deliveries.

The shop was an Aladdin's cave. At the front were shelves were stacked high with animal toys, snacks and nibbles, then farther back birds were perched in cages and colourful fish of all shapes and sizes were swimming in tanks. It was a feast for the senses, a medley of sounds, smells and sights. Several families were huddled around the tanks, staring at the aquatic landscapes that had been created with sunken wrecks and treasure chests. However, my attention was drawn to the small rodents that appeared to be taking part in a range of physical activities, from wheel spinning to running up and down tiny ladders.

Wandering through to the storeroom at the back of the shop, I saw Ted feeding seed to a glorious cockatiel that was perched imperiously on a small stand.

'We are not alone Ted!' It was almost a human voice.

I was shocked by the brazenness of the bird, but Ted laughed as he turned round and explained that this was a party trick it performed whenever they were interrupted. As we shook hands I was taken by the transformation in my friend since our last meeting, several years earlier at a school reunion. His thinning hair and fading smile had been replaced by a luxurious blonde mane and sparkling white teeth that would make an American soap star proud. On his wrist was an expensive Rolex watch and he wore an Armani shirt, open at the neck, revealing a gold chain glistening against his deep tan. Things had certainly been on the up! Then I remembered the Ferrari that was parked outside the frontage I had caught out of the corner of my eye when I entered. Hadn't the number plate been PET 80Y?

'How's things?' It seemed somewhat redundant, but I felt I ought to ask.

'Great, did you see the car?' He smiled showing those teeth. I nodded.

'I couldn't resist that number plate.'

I asked him how what was selling so well in the shop, as I

was intrigued as to what could generate such high income, but he stopped me.

'It's not the shop mate, it's the pets. Take Cocky here for example. He has an audition for a starring role in London next Monday for a gangster film. He has already done other film work. That paid very well.'

He walked back into the shop and pointed to a goldfish swimming on its own in a tank high up on the side aisle.

'That's Buddy. He has just retired. He's done ten years in Coronation Street.'

'Really?' I was fascinated to know what role the goldfish could have had.

'Yes, he's been in Ken Barlow's lounge. Very limited acting needed. But when the camera tracks on him he can be seen swimming up and down or just floating. Basically behaving like a normal goldfish.'

It seemed a pretty easy job to me. But before I could raise this point with him, Ted had already opened a large cage and held a small Syrian hamster in his hand.

'Meet Cyril. Prepare to be impressed.'

With that he cleared a space on the cluttered shelf and placed a large box into which he carefully lowered Cyril. Then he started humming and clapping his hands. The little rodent started jumping up and down from one foot to the other and appeared to be Irish Dancing. It was mesmerising, if not a little uncomfortable to watch.

'He has already starred in several Disney cartoon films. They film him using green screen techniques to create a cartoon over the top. He is a real earner. Cyril comes home with myself and Cocky. I couldn't leave them in the shop. They are my big earners now Buddy has retired. I've just got them in today so I can practice with them. At the moment I am taking Cocky through his lines. It's a big part if he can get it.'

He looked at my expression as I tried to control a fit of laughter.

'You may snigger,' he said, 'but talking birds have lots of lines to learn, like actors. There are several other birds up for this, so he has to be word perfect. Parrots and cockatiels are likely to be there. It's a dog eat dog world in these films!' The mixed metaphor seemed wasted on him.

Looking at my watch I realised that I would need to hot foot it back to pick up my father before he wandered away from the surgery and force me to launch my own missing person investigation. I hadn't even had a chance to ask him about the hair, teeth or that car. Clearly the audition on Monday was a big thing for him, so I wished him luck and agreed not to leave it so long before looking him up next time.

xxx

About a year later I was in the queue at a beer festival back in the town and trying to catch the eye of the old guy in a faded Grateful Dead T shirt serving behind the bar, when a hand was laid on my shoulder. Turning round I saw Ted. He was a shadow of the man I had seen before. Gone were the flash clothes and jewellery and his teeth had long since seen the last of the whitening work. Even his clothes seemed scruffy and worn. I tried to hide my shock at his appearance as I struck up conversation.

'Hey, how's things?' I tried to be as positive as possible.

'Bad. I mean the pet shop is okay, but it's not good with Cocky.'

'Oh dear.' I tried to feign some concern, 'Did he fail the audition.'

'Oh no, he sailed through. He was the best by far. He did a fantastic James Cagney impression, "You dirty rat!" He got the part. '

I was slightly confused. 'So what's the problem? Wasn't that a good role in a movie with a big payout?'

'Sure it was. But he's not with me anymore.'

'You're joking. Oh God, I am sorry to hear that, is he dead?'

'No. Worse than that. He has a new agent and he has moved in with him.'

'Hang on.' I was confused. 'You were his owner. How can he get an agent and leave you.'

'Simple. This guy started talking to him at the audition while we were waiting to leave after he had got the job. I was just getting some more feed and a few special nibbles for him to celebrate. When I came back in the room he said "Ted. I have decided to work with Andrew. Your services are no longer required!"'

'Blimey! The cheek of it!'

'I know, just like that. Well of course I was having none of it and whisked him home. A week later I got a court summons in the post from this guy Andrew Sykes, stating that I was holding the bloody bird against his will!'

'Never!'

'Yep. So I turned up, expecting the whole thing to be laughed out of court. Anyway the judge insisted on questioning Cocky and then said that he thought the bird knew his own mind. In his summing up he said it was clear that the bird wanted to be with Mr Sykes and that I was imprisoning him. That was it. I was given a suspended sentence and a thousand pound fine and the bloody bird now lives with this Sykes guy.'

'I am sorry to hear that Ted.'

'That's not the end of it. The guy has moved here and deliberately keeps bringing the bird into the shop. They always have the same conversation. He says "Does this place look familiar?" and Cocky says "Yes, but I must go. I fear I have developed feelings for Ted when he imprisoned me." And Sykes says "That's Stockholm Syndrome. It's common if you have been held captive".'

Looking at him choking back the tears, I made my excuses and left, reflecting on the whole sad story. On the way out I saw a very tall, smartly dressed man in his fifties seated at a table by the entrance to the medieval hall where the festival was being held. What drew my attention first was the large number of people that surrounded him.

Moving over I saw that it was not the man, but his companion who was drawing the crowd. The beautiful white cockatiel was perched patiently on his outstretched palm. As I moved to the front the bird caught my eye and then, rather wistfully, it looked at the man. In a much less brazen voice than before it quietly squawked 'We are not alone Ted!', looking rather subdued. In turn the man gave the bird a long, rather dreadful and menacing look. I turned and walked away, saddened by the whole spectacle.

Taken for a ride

Marco leant forward in the front seat of his Lancia and took a cigarette from the packet in the glove compartment. He didn't light it. The car was his pride and joy and he didn't allow customers to smoke in it either. Instead he opened the door, got out and rested against the bodywork. Then, after lighting the cigarette, he inhaled and looked out at the view of the Gulf of Naples from the small lay-by. Not a bad place to earn a living he thought. Most of customers were families in the surrounding villages and suburbs wanting lifts into Sorrento for church or the many restaurants. Business was pretty good, but he had to get the car serviced, which cost money and also meant a day's lost income. This was a last stop to reflect before he handed his car over to the local garage to have the work done. He flicked his half smoked cigarette butt over the small wall and brushed the small amount of fallen ash of his freshly pressed slacks.

It was a short drive to the small back street garage in Sant' Agnello where the car would be residing for the next day whilst they replaced the equipment and did a basic service. As he drew up the young mechanic Francesco waved over to him from the edge of the forecourt. The sun-faded sign which had remained untouched for as long as Marco could remember had gone, replaced by a gleaming new Perspex one with a prancing Ferrari horse, presumably to entice luxury car owners.

'Where's Roberto?' Marco asked, after the usual back slapping welcome. He was a regular customer for years now, although he only touched base with them for the annual service.

'Haven't you heard?' Francesco replied 'He sold up a few months ago to a new guy from Naples. Claudio. He's in the office and wants to have a word with you about the work.'

'What! It's just a standard service!' Marco raised his eyes upwards impatiently as he strolled over to Roberto's old office. Although he was a short man, Marco had an imposing air, partly due to the swaggering gait he employed when walking. Looking around he could see that the garage bore scant resemblance to the disorganised family business he had known so well. Gone were the flashy calendars, discarded empty oil cans and used threadbare tyres, replaced instead by the air of an efficient and sanitised work environment. Reaching the office, he knocked and entered in the same movement. As he opened the door a short wiry man in a smart blue suit turned around quickly. He had jet black hair greased down and wore designer aviator shades.

'Marco, Claudio nice to meet you.' He held out his hand and Marco shook it. 'I just wanted to make you aware that we are fixing additional security features especially for taxis-the same that we do in our Naples garage. A bullet proof glass window between you and the passengers for your safety. You can't be too sure, lots of guns around these days.' He smiled as he lingered on the last few words, displaying some expensive dental work. 'For you as a valued old customer, we can do it for a reduced price; just three thousand euros.'

Marco stared at the man; he was not sure if he was hearing correctly. Normally he paid one hundred euros for a service. This was way out of his league. Dino and Mama Fittipaldi would hardly pull a gun on him when being driven to church or picked up from a restaurant.

'No thanks, just the annual service.' He replied dismissively.

'OK. Sure. No pressure. Of course, it's your choice.' Claudio smiled and turned away.

After handing over the keys and stressing to Francesco that he just wanted the usual service Marco strolled off back to his apartment, agreeing to pick up the Lancia the next day. He whistled contentedly to himself. Really, did they really think I'd fall for paying that much, he thought. Maybe in Naples, but not here. No way!

xxx

After his second coffee and third cigarette, and having read most of the paper outside the local cafe a short walk from his home, Marco received a text from the garage letting him know that the Lancia was ready for collection. He smiled to himself when he thought how less discerning drivers may have been persuaded by what he was now convinced was clearly a scam.

When he arrived at the garage there was no sign of either Francesco or the new owner Claudio. Instead a thick set man with the physique of a wrestler in mechanic's overalls was installing what appeared to be one of the new bulletproof screens into a Mercedes taxi with a Naples number plate. Barely raising his head, he grunted a brief acknowledgement and threw Marco the keys with a nod.

It was good to get his taxi back and he went for a drive down the Amalfi coast as he had no pickups scheduled until after lunch. He wound the window down and smelt the fresh breeze against his face as he drove south from Sorrento on the Corso Italia. The engine purred and the car cruised smoothly along the open road. The service had clearly breathed new life into his old car. However, the traffic soon ground to a halt as he approached the turning for Amalfi itself and so he retreated from the lunchtime rush hour to a small roadside cafe run by an old friend. Marco noticed his favourite table was free, outside in the shade, with breathtaking views to the sea.

He nodded to Luca and was just entering the establishment to order his third coffee of the morning, when his mobile vibrated. Looking at the screen he saw an unknown number. He knew this was not one of his normal clients, as he had given himself time off until his afternoon bookings to allow for collecting the car. However, the annual service needed to be paid for, so tentatively he answered the phone. A sultry female asked if she could have a taxi in thirty minutes from a block of new maisonettes in San Pietro, for a drop off at the Parco Lauro in Sorrento. Reluctantly, he realised it made sense to take the fare as it was back in his normal work patch. So, after making an apologetic gesture to his friend, Marco drove in the opposite direction back down the road.

The block was in a quiet backstreet and he had been waiting a minute or so, when a glamorous woman in her mid thirties in designer clothing strolled up and got into the back of the taxi. She looked like a model with her flowing hair and elaborate make up Marco thought to himself, as he flashed his best smile.

'Piazza Angelina Lauro!' her voice was hard and abrupt.

He nodded and drove on. This was clearly going to be a trip with limited or no conversation. The traffic was beginning to clog as lunchtime approached and Marco used his best local knowledge to navigate the blocked roads via a number of backstreets- not that his passenger showed any appreciation of this fact. Eventually the taxi purred into the square and pulled into a parking bay in front of Banco Sella.

'Wait here!' she instructed, getting out and crossing the road to enter a small fashion boutique.

Marco considered getting out and having another cigarette. However, unsure if she may be back in a few minutes, he checked his phone for messages and then turned the local radio on low instead. He stroked the steering wheel and patted the dashboard of his Lancia. The car had served him well and he considered it a faithful friend.

After a few minutes he heard the door slam behind him and a deep voice grunted 'Drive!' Looking in the rear view mirror he saw a large man wearing a bright green 'incredible hulk' mask, with a baseball cap on his head. In his hand was a small revolver, pointing at the base of Marco's neck.

How could he have been so stupid, he had been warned and had the chance to buy the bullet proof glass partition! Instead he had dismissed the offer out of hand. Well, this will teach me, he thought. This must be a robbery! They were right outside the bank and the man appeared to be cradling a sports holdall, presumably containing the stolen money, on his lap.

'Drive!!' the man grunted more urgently, now pressing the cold metal of the end of the gun barrel hard against Marco's skin.

'OK, where?' he stammered, slamming the car into gear and swerving it into the road before picking up speed.

The next thirty minutes were a blank as he was directed to

drive round an increasing complex maze of streets and narrow alleys, until he was told to pull up behind the refuse bins at the back of a local disused restaurant. He nearly crashed twice as the man made the gun nozzle snuggle against his neck and shouted for him to drive faster. As he sped past the front of L'Antica Trattoria, he had seen Francesco and Luisa Conte waving frantically, attempting to call him for a taxi home.

His poor Lancia had not experienced this type of driving before. My beloved car, he thought, as he had thrashed the gears and screamed the tyres following the man's barked commands. Finally, the man jumped out and ran off at high speed beyond a small unimposing block of apartments.

xxx

Marco didn't sleep much that night. He woke several times in a hot sweat just thinking of how close he had come to being shot. He remonstrated with himself over how foolish he had been to not get the work done when he had the chance. After all, you could not put a price on life preservation and he vowed to himself to book the car in the very next day. It would be another day when he was not earning and he would have to cancel a few regular bookings at the last minute, but this now seemed pretty insignificant.

Driving round to the garage his mind kept flashing back

to the day before. Something was not quite right, but he just couldn't put his finger on it. He decided not to phone, but instead turned up when the garage opened. Fortunately, given his persistence and the cash he handed over, it was slotted in straightaway that morning. As he walked away his eye caught a bright green piece of fabric glowing in the bin amongst the oily rags and he felt a little uneasy.

Later, finishing his coffee in a nearby cafe while he waited for the work on the car to be completed, he remembered the thought that had been nagging away all day. At no point had he seen anyone come out of the bank chasing the bank robber and there was no evidence of any police car, even unmarked, on his trail whilst he drove around with the gun at his neck for that half hour. Indeed, there had been no mention of the robbery on the local news.

This made him feel even more uneasy. Lighting his cigarette he leaned back and surveyed the view. As he looked out at the busy scene, with the boats and cars ferrying people to the tourist destinations along the coast, Marco couldn't help thinking that he himself had been taken for a ride.

Picture This!

'Take it here!' he shouted as she looked up to see him perched at the top of a large pillar in Trafalgar Square.

'Next to the lion?'

'Yeah. But wait for it.'

With that he stretched himself out and upwards into a perfect handstand. It was a long way down. A very long way down to hard stone. The couple who were sitting at the foot of the pillar, and who would have cushioned his fall, had just moved away in slight alarm. A few people had stopped and were looking over in his direction. Then he slowly raised one arm. Somehow he was balanced on just a single hand by the way he had moved his body. He gave out a loud yell. Then she took the picture.

'Fantastic' he said looking at the phone five minutes later as they ate their burgers and sucked a shared coke through their two straws. 'Now upload it to Instagram and Twitter.'

'And Facebook?'

'Go on then' he shrugged begrudgingly, before handing the phone over. Her hands weaved their magic on the screen.

Finished, they threw their rubbish in a bin. The phone started buzzing.

'You've got a hundred likes already' she said, eyes wide in

amazement.

'You know me love. Always give them what they want.'

'Where now?'

'Wait and see!'

xxx

As they crossed the bridge, they could see the glass edifice of the Shard rise up above them.

'Bloody Hell. Are you going to climb that? Not from the outside surely?' she looked at him, alarmed.

'Nah, don't be stupid. I'm going go up to the top of the bloody thing in the lift and then I'll fake a selfie leaning out of the window.'

'Really, will the windows open?'

'Watch and learn, watch and learn!'

They entered the building through the glass doors into the smart foyer and joined the short queue for the lift. A few minutes later they were up on the fifty-second floor and lined up outside the entrance of the bar. Before she knew it he was off and heading in the direction of the toilets. As the line snaked forwards she wondered if he would be back in time before she was greeted. Then there was a tap on her back.

'Come on', he winked. 'We're all done here!'

It was disappointing as she would have liked to have stayed for a drink and admire the view, but something in his urgency made her not question their departure. Outside around the small plaza he gleefully showed her the photo.

'Blimey, how did you get that?'

There was a bird's eye view down from the floor, all fifty-two stories.

'Easy, just used this.' He pulled a small black telescopic selfie stick out of the pocket of his padded jacket. 'My new toy! I found a tiny part of a window in the toilets that opened just enough to get it through and pointing down.'

Ten minutes later they had uploaded the photo and had taken the tube back home.

xxx

He went out on his own that night and came in at just after two in the morning. He was buzzing.

'You should have seen it. We recorded it! I jumped the tracks. You know, on the tube.'

'What? Where?' She was shocked that he had done something so dangerous, even for him.

'Just on the track coming into Bank station. Nobody was there and it was a straight jump across. You've just got to make about eight or nine feet. Look at the footage. It's pretty tight. Just two of us attempted it.'

He showed and she couldn't believe it. In fact, she looked away. This was too irresponsible. She told him she refused to upload it, but he told her Tony had done it on Youtube anyway and it had hit a thousand already. They argued and he slept on the old couch in the lounge, after he had thrown all the dirty clothes off it and managed to rearrange the cushions. Relenting she gave him the blankets and sheet off the bed, whilst she kept the duvet.

xxx

The next morning she had already decided what needed to be done. She had to break this fascination he had. So she suggested they take a trip out. What about the seaside? He didn't like this but they came up with the compromise of a walk on the cliffs at Beachy Head. He had heard of it and about the high cliffs with the drop below.

They caught the main line train down from Waterloo station to Seaford and after a short taxi journey were at the car park at the foot of the coastal path. It was a beautiful day and the cliff walk towered above them. She pointed out the famous Seven Sisters to him. He bounded up the path, overtaking the leisure walkers with a fierce sense of purpose. Within minutes they approached the highest point, with the lighthouse standing proudly on the rocks below. Already there was a queue of tourists standing close to the edge, posing with the sea and sky behind. They moved slowly forward, but she could sense his resentment that this held no special challenge with the mass participation they were witnessing.

Then suddenly she saw his eyes blaze as an idea took seed.

'Come on!' He led her beyond the group to a small promontory further along the path, jutting out over the beach below.

'No!'

She stopped and called him back, but he already had the selfie stick out of his pocket and was attaching his phone to the end of it. Then he extended the telescopic section so that the camera lens was a good four foot from his hand. On his hands and knees he crawled in his bright yellow coat towards the edge, like a crustacean with one long tentacle. Unlike the safer position where the others were taking photos, this was much riskier. The edge of the cliff had been about five foot away when he first lowered himself onto the turf and soon he was looking down at the choppy sea lapping the pebble beach.

Of course she knew he would not stop at this point. That was far too conventional. It was no surprise when she saw the camera slowly extend beyond the edge, still parallel to the ground. At this point a crowd of bystanders had gathered a short distance back on the cliff path, transfixed by the possibility of impending disaster. This was what he thrived on she realised. To scare people. To make them take a step back and retreat back into the norm.

And so, as he fell and the screams echoed around, people frantically calling on the mobiles for the police, paramedics and coastguard, she stood there calmly knowing that he had found peace with the ultimate prize. First place in the shock category, she thought to herself. Perhaps somebody on the beach below had the ultimate shock as he came hurtling down towards them, the extended arm stretched behind from the drag force.

Later, in the police car, drinking tea from a policewoman's flask, she wondered what was next. They had taken his body away. She had not seen it, but she had overheard one of the paramedics saying it 'looked like a starfish' when he landed. He would have liked that. To go out memorably. She had his phone, which had been found a little way away from his body, fully dislocated from its metal arm. If there were any photos that could be extracted then she would upload them, as a tribute.

xxx

Getting off the return train later, she walked back to the small unwelcoming flat alone. A loud roar came from behind her as a motorcyclist overtook several cars and weaved in and out of the traffic, defying the rush hour stalemate. Half a mile later she walked up to him where he had pulled the bike over.

'Cool riding' she called over smiling.

'Yeah- fancy a ride?' He threw her a crash helmet.

'Great.' She jumped on the back of the bike, wrapping her arms around his chest. I don't even know him, she thought, as they drove off.

At the cafe they sat on the bench in the sun, their helmets beside them as they drunk the coffees she had bought. He rubbed the back of his long brown hair and squinted at her through his aviator shades. He looks pretty cool she thought. Holding the phone away from her, she photographed the two of them.

'So you'd be happy to photo me on the bike?' he said, innocently, a while later.

'No problem. You've jumped before? I mean proper jumping over ramps, you know?'

'Well, yeah! I don't know, maybe I could clear a few buses.' he laughed. 'That would be a thrill! And you could photo me.'

'Yeah, maybe.' She turned away, smiling. The next project was sorted.

The Protest

Sandra sighed as she sat herself down behind the teacher's desk, watching the class shuffle out of the door. They weren't so bad really. Jasbinder had shown real promise today and had explained the circle theorems very succinctly to the rest of the class. What a pity Warren Smith on the back row had tried to stir up the less-motivated students. 'Playing to the gallery', she called it. Never mind, she must get going. This was her half day and she had to hot foot it to the station to get the fast train into town to join the protest. She smiled as she thought of meeting Jan and Smudge again. Smudge was a little wild in his ideas, but harmless enough and Jan kept him in his place. Looking around she was surprised to see the classroom looked relatively unscathed; they had even managed to put the chairs back where she had asked them. Neatly arranging her desk ready for the next day, she switched the light off, descended the concrete stairs and exited the school building.

Breathless from the short run, Sandra arrived on the platform and checked the contents of her rucksack, namely a flask of tea, a round of salad sandwiches and a rolled up banner proclaiming "Tackle Climate Change NOW!" She had initially considered a wearing a rainbow coloured bandana she had kept from her student protest days, but at nearly sixty she dismissed this as a ridiculous notion. Looking around, she saw there were only a few other passengers waiting on the platform of the small single-line station. She wondered to herself if any of them were going to protest. On first glance it seemed unlikely.

Ten minutes later, Sandra sat at a table seat as the villages and fields sped by, like a moving landscape painting framed by the carriage window. A young woman in her early twenties, sat in the seat opposite, nodding her head, presumably in time to music on her headphones. Unlike at rush hour, the train was about half full. She smiled at the girl, who reminded her of herself at that age, so idealistic and free from the constraints that bind us in later life. The girl caught her out of the corner of her eye and briefly nodded an acknowledgement. The train became more crowded as it got closer to Bristol and soon a smartly dressed young man dropped himself down in the adjoining seat to Sandra. Normally she drove into the city's suburbs to visit her elderly mother at this time each week, but she had phoned through with the excuse of a doctor's appointment. She couldn't face the derisory comments that would flow if she mentioned attending the rally.

'Aren't you a bit old to be taken in by all that rubbish!'

She snapped out of her thoughts and turned to see the smartly dressed young man next to her staring at the banner which protruded slightly from her the front pocket of her rucksack. Sandra flushed.

'I thought it was the younger generation who actually understood the consequences of our actions on the climate.' She replied, tersely.

'Not me, love.' He smiled, showing perfect white teeth. 'I sell cars. It's all claptrap. You should listen to Trump, he talks some sense.'

Sandra felt like exploding at the mere mention of the name. In an effort to regain some composure and defuse the situation, she replied. 'Well, we will just have to agree to disagree on that one. It is a democracy last time I checked and we are all free to have our own opinions.'

The girl opposite had removed her headphones and was looking over at the two passengers opposite.

'True, but just don't tell me you are one of those activists who lie down in the road and hold up all the traffic, making it a nightmare for us commuters.' He barked.

Sandra grimaced, and looked away.

'Oh no, you are, aren't you? Really! I don't believe it.' He turned to address the passengers in the near vicinity. 'Hey, she wants to block the roads in Bristol city centre this afternoon. What do you think of that?' he snarled.

There was a general mummer of discontent, accompanied by several shouts of 'Shame!', 'Bloody idiot', 'Get a job!' and the like. An old man a few seats back sarcastically whistled the old labour anthem 'Red Flag!' which was met with further jeering.

Sandra shifted uncomfortably in her seat. Sadly she could not see any of the other activists in the carriage who could come to her defence and she began to feel completely isolated. It was at this point, presumably sensing the growing atmosphere, that the girl opposite turned and spoke loudly to Sandra.

'Well I admire this you for the stance you're making. I think that we all need to be aware of climate change and what we can do to reduce the effects of it. The government doesn't seem to care, so good on you for protesting.'

'Ridiculous' muttered the young man and several others also spoke under their breath. But it seemed to silence most of the passengers.

Sandra smiled over at the girl, but she was relieved to see that they had pulled into Temple Meads station, and after hanging back until the train had emptied, on the pretence of checking her purse, she dismounted herself, walking head down to the agreed rendezvous point for the protest on Spike Island.

xxx

'What do we want?' A scrawny middle aged man with a shaggy beard and ponytail shouted into a megaphone.

'Tackle climate change!' the growing crowd of protestors

shouted back.

'When do we want it?'

'Now!!'

Sandra joined in with gusto waving her banner and standing side by side with Jan. Smudge had moved right to the front and was waving making an obscene gesture to a young police officer with one hand, while holding the cup of coffee he was swigging from in the other. The crowd surged forward against the giant reptile created by the police riot shields. Somebody threw a bottle which smashed against the police van parked at the junction of the main street. The noise was greeted by a loud cheer. The police responded by pushing the protestors back using the shields. A group of teenagers in the crowd to the left of her shouted that they had seen a water cannon ready to be deployed. Looking nervously towards the frontline of the action, Sandra hoped she couldn't see Dan, a policeman who she knew from quiz nights at her local pub.

Sandra felt the sense of excitement as the crowd started chanting once again. She recognised faces in the crowd around her from previous protests. Delving into her rucksack, she withdrew the now squashed sandwiches, offering one to Jan. She refused, but Smudge leaned over and grabbed it rather unceremoniously out of Sandra's hand. She was just sharing the tea from her flask with Jan when she felt something vibrate in her pocket. Bugger! She had

forgotten to turn her phone off! Looking down she saw her
brother appear as the contact. Reluctantly she moved away
from Jan, hoping that they would not get separated in the
flowing tide of protestors.

'Hi Marc.' Her tone was brusque. He was the last person
she wanted to speak to today.

'Where are you? Don't you usually see mum today?'

'Well yes I do.' I see her more often than you with your
busy life and no time to get away, she thought. 'I told her I
couldn't make it today as I had a doctor's appointment. I
phoned through and told her earlier. Why?'

'Well mum's had a fall and she's conscious, but confused.'
He continued. 'A neighbour called me, as they couldn't get
through to you.' He let this hang in the air for a few seconds.
She looked down and swore silently as she saw the missed
call.

'Anyway, they're waiting for an ambulance, but they can't
get through at the moment as these bloody stupid protestors
have blocked the roads. The centre of Bristol is gridlock
apparently.' He paused to draw breath. 'Anyway, where are
you? It's sounds noisy.'

'Just near the doctor's surgery. Let me know where they
take her. Please Marc.' Jan arrived by her side as she ended
the call.

'Come on, you're missing the good bit.' Jan updated her.
'Smudge has hit an officer with a bottle he threw and some

businessmen in suits have come out to support the police. Get waving that banner Sandra! Stop climate change NOW!!'

Sandra felt a little sick inside with worry. She wasn't sure if her heart was in the protest anymore. Still she waved the banner with as much gusto as she could generate in the circumstances.

'What about the ambulances for emergencies?' She asked a while later.

'Tough!' Jan's words stung her.

Shards of water cascaded over her as the police fired the water canon in the direction of the protestors. Smudge, now more incensed than ever, was hurling every item he could find in their general direction. He looked ridiculous, Sandra thought. And out of breath and with a florid complexion; this was clearly the only exercise he ever did and it was taking its toll!

Her phone vibrated again and ignoring the noise she took it straightaway, without attempting to move to somewhere quieter.

'Marc! Has the ambulance got there yet?'

'Yes, panic over. They have treated mum and she doesn't need to go to hospital. They think it was a panic attack, rather than a heart attack.'

'That's great news. Thanks for letting me know.'

'What's that noise? Are you near the protest?'

'Yes, it's near the surgery. Speak soon.'

She hung up and nodded at Jan who was waving over to her.

'What is it Jan?'

'They've got a problem. A girl has been hit by the missiles. She looks bad, it's not good.'

Sandra started to say 'Where's the ambulance?', but her voice trailed off as she moved forward and could see Jasbinder lying on the pavement with a small pool of blood by her head. Leaning over her, clearly distraught, Sandra recognised her mother, Mrs Singh, from parents' evening. Strewn across the pavement where plastic bags full of shopping from an afternoon spent in the city centre. Checking her watch, she realised it was now past five o'clock and they must have caught a later train after school.

'Get an ambulance!!' Sandra shouted urgently, trying to push to the front of the crowd.

Smudge stared at her. 'An ambulance! Don't be ridiculous Sandra. Are you mad? This is what we wanted. We're making our point and the publicity from this will be massive. Ambulances can't get through to her anyway. I think they are trying to land the air ambulance on the top level of that multi-storey over there.' He pointed to the Rupert Street Car Park. 'She should be all right.' He added graciously as an afterthought.

Sandra felt distraught. If there was any student she felt an affinity to it was Jasbinder Singh. Unlike the majority of the class, she showed a real interest and was a pleasure to teach. Moving closer to the frontline of the protest, she could see that paramedics were taking the small body on a stretcher back to the waiting helicopter. Her mother was walking beside them, crying and holding Jasbinder's hand. She felt relief flood through her body. Hopefully the girl would be fine.

xxx

The protest began to increase in volume and numbers. This was now peak rush hour time and several TV reporters could be seen giving their news feed reports from sheltered locations beside the police lines. Suddenly, there was a loud thud and a scream right behind her and turning she saw a distraught Jan leaning over Smudge. At first she thought he had tripped, but then she saw him pulling at his throat, trying to breathe. His face was now a pallid white and he was sweating profusely. It looked like he was having a heart attack. Jan was cradling his head as he lay prostrate on the ground.

'Somebody call 999. Quick- he's struggling to breathe!'

There was a horrible noise as the gasps became more desperate.

Eventually Sandra got through. In the meantime the police had tried to stop the helicopter taking off, but it was already airborne. An ambulance would be on its way, but they could not give a precise arrival time. 'The centre of Bristol is in lockdown because of the protest', the call handler told her, even after she had explained the casualty was one of the protestors.

Jan looked up as she relayed the news.

'He's really not looking good. He'll be okay won't he Sandra?' Tears welled in her eyes. At that moment a protestor using the megaphone, gave details of tomorrow's protest in Bath.

Sandra bit her lip.

Road Rage

Ever since attending the 1912 Motor cycle and Cycle car show in Olympia, he had set his heart on the new Little Midland, open body, two-seater. It was one of the first cycle cars to have been manufactured in England and had benefitted from the production of only one model giving it the company's full focus. The production numbers would be low, but he put down the full price of one hundred guineas there and then to the gentleman at the company stand. Now, five months later, the car was finally arriving today on the bullet steam train at Henley on Thames. The engineer, who he would meet at the station, would then take him for an orientation drive before handing the vehicle over and being dropped back to catch the return train. Mathers, his most trusted and longest serving tenant farmer, was bringing him into Henley from his Hambeldon estate in his horse and cart. It was a fresh summer day and Mathers talked excitedly about the new purchase.

'Yes sir, I gather it's for touring you see rather than racing, so it will be just the ticket to drive yourself and the lady up to Oxford or down to London. Built for comfort, rather than speed.'

'Yes Mathers. I really am very keen to get my hands on her. She looked lovely at the show last year.'

He rearranged his deerstalker and the thick tweed great coat he had taken the precaution to wear. Underneath he had a woollen jumper and plus fours. Although he had never driven a cycle car before, the advice in his paper was that shooting gear was the best for comfort and to protect against the elements. Reluctantly, he accepted the separation from his beloved briar pipe, normally a permanent feature hanging from his mouth, often unlit, for most of his waking hours.

The powerful carthorse made good time, trotting along the narrow lanes towards Henley. He looked around him on either side. There really could be no more beautiful views in England than the Oxfordshire countryside at this time of year, he thought to himself. There were lush green fields as far as the eye could see, punctuated by thick copses of healthy beach trees and the occasional small stream. Mathers dropped his landowner off at the small station and headed back to his farm on the estate, leaving him on the platform in a high state of anticipation to wait for the delivery.

Within twenty minutes, the small train pulled in with a few passenger carriages and then the freight carriage with the large delivery covered by tarpaulin, tied down with ships knots. A young rotund man with a pasty complexion jumped down from the carriage and introduced himself as Percy Stubbs, one of the design engineers at Little Midland or LM as the company was known. Stubbs looked like he has spent too much time behind a drawing board and not enough in the outdoors, he thought to himself. Indeed, the grimy fingernails and unpolished shoes suggested a man more used to the factory floor than entertaining wealthy clients.

'Yours is only the sixth this year and two of those went abroad sir!' Stubbs informed him excitedly as they shook hands.

He was man of integrity and humility, but the sight of the beautiful silver cycle car was too much. As it was taken off the low loader and on to the end of the platform he could not resist a glow of pride to think that he owned one of the only four cars in England. After several minutes undoing the ropes and checking the vehicle was fully intact and roadworthy, Stubbs jumped into the driver's seat and gestured for him to sit next to him. The seats themselves were thick brown leather and felt as comfortable as his favourite armchair in the drawing room by the fire. In fact, he realised he would need to concentrate fully, if he was to avoid drifting into the light slumber he found so easy most afternoons.

'Just a short lesson sir if you don't mind. Can I assume that you won't be taking the cycle car into any large towns or into London yet?' Stubbs' voice jerked him out of his thoughts.

'Oh no. Just locally along the country lanes for the foreseeable future, Mr Stubbs.'

'That is very wise sir. There are more and more motor

bikes and cycle cars in the large towns and cities these days. We have had reports of queues at the road junctions and tempers can fray easily. Now I will give you the basics to drive, steer, accelerate and stop. We will also go through parking and using the road junctions. My return train is not for three hours, so that should be enough time if you would be kind enough to take me back to the station later.'

The time flew by and soon he had full mastery of the vehicle. It was relatively simple, he thought to himself, as he found the Little Midland surprisingly powerful, with a good turn of speed and acceleration. His choice of clothing had been wise, as the car moved through the air much faster than the horse and cart, and the chill bit his face. After returning Mr Stubbs back to the railway station, he opened the throttle. His senses thrilled to the sweet smell of the hedge flowers that scuttled by, combined with the loud roar of the engine. Aware of the limited fuel capacity, he made just one stop to visit the faithful Mathers. As he drove into the farmyard, the old man came out to see him, waving his cap in the air.

'Well sir. She is as beautiful as they said in the newspaper. The star of last year's show.'

'Yes, she is a beauty isn't she?' He blushed a little at the thought that he could own such a car. Mathers never could of course, he reminded himself. Saying his goodbyes he drove the short distance back to his imposing Queen Anne manor house and parked the car securely in his large barn for the night. Before retiring, he filled the petrol tank up using fuel he stored in cans.

xxx

The next morning straight after breakfast, he decided to take the Little Midland out on a longer drive. Armed with a flask of tea and wearing a thick overcoat, driving gloves, hat and goggles, he set off through the village, waving to the locals who were tending to the fields. Old Mrs Jones, the postmistress curtseyed as he whizzed past the village green. The schoolchildren who were walking by the side of the road stopped and their teacher Mr Gallagher lined them all up against the fence as they waved to him. Some of the children shouted excitedly, they had never seen such a vehicle before.

Young Geordie Brown, the baker's son, called out cheekily, 'Give us a ride sir!'

The other children cheered as, perhaps against his better judgement, he let Geordie jump on board and sit in the seat next to him. He took him for a short drive through the village to the vicarage and back again. Geordie waved frantically to the other children, beaming with pride as the car growled when he changed gear. As they turned, he took his eyes off the road and saw Geordie fiddling around under the dashboard. When the boy caught him looking, he jumped back sheepishly. On the drive back, the boy was very silent.

'What's the matter Geordie?' he asked.

'Nothing sir. Thanks for the ride!' He said jumping out once they had stopped, to cheers from his peers.

He then drove up the narrow lane to the imposing manor house, where his friend Fitzpatrick-Lucy lived. He swept the cycle car through the gates and along the tree lined drive, stopping on the gravel outside the impressive facade. Like him, Fitzpatrick-Lucy lived off his investments and spent most of his time at home, unless he was visiting his brokers in London. His friend was working in his study, but raised the window as he heard the engine and called to him.

'What a beauty, what a fantastic vehicle!'

Fitzpatrick-Lucy bounded out through the entrance. After several minutes admiring the bodywork, he was soon seated alongside his friend.

'I say sir! May I have a ride around the grounds in this beautiful beast?'

He nodded his head in ascent and they shot of up the drive and veered off to take in the small boating lake. From there they headed to the field where the game shooting was held, briefly stopping for a smoke while they discussed the next event in the season. Ten minutes later he had waved goodbye.

Away from the village, he found the Little Midland travelled at a modest speed, but that was still about three times the speed of a horse and cart and soon he was approaching Mathers' farm, which was on the boundary edge of his estate. He could see cattle slowly turning their disinterested heads as he passed and then in the next field foals cantering alongside the fence, overtaking him with ease.

It was as he was exiting a slow bend that he became aware of something to the rear in the distance when looking into the side mirror. He checked using the cabin mirror and was astonished to see another cycle car approaching from behind. It was bright red and looked similar to his Little Midland. Bugger, he thought. He certainly did not expect anybody else to be driving a cycle car in these local villages. He was unaware of any other people of similar wealth who could afford such a vehicle, so he assumed that it must be an outsider from a neighbouring county.

Looking back in the mirror, he saw that the car was now gaining on him. It was the latest Alfa Romeo. A faster, foreign model that was only available via an expensive and complex import procedure, he had read in The Times that it was becoming a fixture on the emerging racing circuits. For these reasons he had dismissed any intention of purchasing one himself.

'Move over, won't you?' An American voice shouted.

A stout middle-aged man with a cigar in his mouth was gesturing angrily from the passenger seat of the Alfa Romeo, which was now less than a car length behind. He wore a racing cap and a tweed cloak was wrapped around his shoulders. Next to him in similar garb, was a younger man, perhaps early twenties, with wild eyes, who was revving the car to its maximum break horse power.

'I say,' he said. 'just wait behind will you, until we get past this corner.'

'No way buddy. Move over, I said!'

He could now see the car had gained on him and was now side by side as they entered the tight corner.

'This is madness!' He called out.

He went to press the horn. Nothing! Looking down now he could see the rubber bulb had come away from the metal frame. That bloody Geordie Brown he thought. That's why he was so bloody subdued. He broke it with his fiddling!

Looking across he could see that the American was gesturing to him to slow down and let them pass. But why should he give way, he thought to himself. What a bloody cheek! He felt his temper rise. After all, this was his land. These roads ran through his estate and he owned most of the farms and cottages in the villages. How dare the American speak to him in this way!

At that moment a familiar sight came into view on the other side of the road facing the Alfa Romeo. Mathers sat astride his cart, with the horse in front trotting patiently towards them, directly in the path of the oncoming Americans as they attempted to overtake. This was a scene that had repeated itself every day since Mathers had taken up the tenancy many years ago, when he had first acquired the estate.

'Cut in behind me!' he cried out to the other driver.

'No way buddy. You give way!' The American was puffing madly on the cigar and patting his driver on the back with encouragement.

The cars were now less than twenty feet from Mathers and the horse. He looked into the confused eyes of his friend. There was nothing for it. He slammed on the breaks of the Little Midland, allowing the shining Alfa Romeo to glide through the gap that opened and disappear into the distance, with only the honk of the horn as an acknowledgement.

The breaking was too sharp of course. He knew this. The car veered to the right, crashing through the wire fence that separated the field from the lane. Landing in a small ditch, used to catch the runoff from the field, the wheels buckled and the gleaming silver body shuddered and then broke in several places. He managed to climb out fairly easily, apparently completely unscathed. The mangled body of his beloved Little Midland was clearly damaged beyond repair.

Turning around sheepishly, he saw his old friend astride his cart stationary in the lane shaking his head in bewilderment. A deep sense of embarrassment flooded over him, as catching his eye, Mathers turned away.

Radio

'Can I just say what a pleasure it is to chat to you, Professor Howard Boner. Our listeners have got a little more insight into the back story to a well-known inventor and academic. As we mentioned earlier, your latest invention, the Boner Solar Radio has been getting early rave reviews.'

'Yes, I am proud of our new radio. It has already been adopted by some UK aid agencies and shipped to several third world countries. Of course, we have reduced the production cost to such a low level, just two pounds, allowing worldwide access.' He looked away. He wasn't going to explain that the cost was now under a pound, making his company a pound profit for each radio sold. For Howard had a tendency to pomposity and colleagues whispered behind his back about his inflated sense of self-importance.

'Now, which of the ten songs you have chosen would be the one desert island disc you would take with you?'

'Because I am a rebel at heart, I would have to choose Holidays in the Sun, by the Sex Pistols'

'And which luxury item would you take?'

'Well, as you know, I feel that the power of radio allows those of us who inhabit the most remote places access to global civilisation, so I would say the Boner Solar Radio.'

'Once again, thank you very much for appearing on

Desert Island Discs this week.'

'Thank you, it has been a pleasure.'

As the familiar music faded in, signalling the end of the show, Howard shook hands with the young female presenter and made his way out of the studio. Moving down the stairs he handed over the temporary pass at reception and headed to the nearest pub for a quick pint.

Seated at a table in the deserted bar area with a pint of Whitstable Bay on the table in front of him, Howard took out his phone and checked for messages. There was a text from his partner wishing him well with his appearance on the show and another from the airline confirming his flight details for the conference he was attending in the Bahamas the next day. Better have just the one drink he thought and have a clear head to avoid forgetting anything important for the trip.

He replied to his partner. It was a long distance relationship and it suited him that way. He could enjoy her company at the restaurant or theatre, but Howard didn't have her nagging him as he balanced his tea on his lap and dropped food down his front while watching the TV.

xxx

At the airport, Howard checked in and made his way to the first class lounge to wait patiently for the flight call. When he had first travelled in business class, to an international seminar as a young lecturer making his way in academia, he had been struck by how different it was to his previous economy ticket experience. Now he took the free nibbles, papers and drinks for granted as he mingled with similar professionals. It was clear to Howard that he was at the top of his game, both within the university and the wider academic world. It would be fair to say his position was unassailable. Indeed, so rapt was the attention of the students in his lectures, as they hung on every word, that he often considered adding some gibberish, confident that it would be accepted verbatim.

Howard felt he deserved the business executive lifestyle as a reward for his life's commitment to his field of study. Generally he would not consider himself ostentatious in any way and the clothes he wore to conferences always looked like they had come from a charity shop rather than an upmarket gents outfitters, like some of his colleagues of similar standing. Several of his peers even drove the latest Tesla models and he was aware how much they cost! In fact he was generally a frugal man who did not own a car and lived a small flat, but first class travel and dining out were his only indulgences. It was a fact not wasted on his Head of Faculty, who received the large invoices after each business trip, but offset these against the very large research funding Howard's work generated. He was now working on launching the solar radio in the UK, although privately he was having second thoughts about the 'It's a Boner!' marketing campaign that the young sales executives had championed so enthusiastically. Indeed, it had met with several howls of derision amongst the exclusive pseudo Bloomsbury crowd he inhabited within the upmarket area of the medieval city he called home.

Howard grabbed an espresso and a bowl of mixed nuts, before settling down in a deep leather armchair in a quiet corner of the cavernous room. In his attaché case he had his laptop and also a working Boner Solar Radio. He had uploaded his technical files and the presentation file to the company cloud storage facility ready to access during his talk. Although the radio had been championed by several overseas aid charities, it did not have a particularly high international profile. This conference, led by several major aid organisations and representatives from interested governments, was the opportunity to change all of that. His assistant had forwarded him the good reviews in the national press of the previous day's radio programme, which had been aired a few hours after it had been recorded.

The call came through for his flight and within a few minutes he was seated several rows back from the front of business class. Glad of the lightweight linen suit he always wore for travelling, he loosened his tie and removed his old scuffed loafers. The seat was wide and had enough legroom for Howard to stretch his relatively short legs and doze, until an air steward interrupted him to confirm his meal choices.

The wide variety and better quality of the food was another perk he enjoyed from this class of travel. Howard ordered a double gin and tonic and then sat back to examine the brochure he had been sent, outlining the conference centre and accommodation. As usual, he had been booked into a junior suite with sea views from its wide terrace. Although Howard would be working hard, he was looking forward to swimming in the large infinity pool and relaxing at the many shore side bars the hotel offered.

Making good time, the aircraft was cruising towards its destination, when Howard first sensed something might be wrong. As a seasoned traveller with a large carbon footprint that was the envy of many of his university colleagues, he was used to the steady drone of a healthy aircraft in flight. The noise the plane was beginning to make now was not one he had heard before and he became aware that several other passengers were also starting to look concerned.

Looking back, Howard realised that it all happened in just a few minutes. First the cabin was plunged into darkness, accompanied by a cacophony of shouts and screams. Then the plane lurched in several random directions, whilst the passengers tried to stay seated, rather like cowboys in a rodeo show, as personal belongings were thrown all around them. Finally, part of the fuselage was ripped off with a horrendous low pitched growl, leaving them exposed to the icy breath of the atmosphere at several thousand feet above the now clearly visible water.

Sensing a crash was imminent, Howard placed himself in the brace position wearing the life preserver. After that there was nothing. Then less than a minute later, accompanied by the sound of frantic prayers, the plane made impact with the Caribbean Sea.

xxx

When he came round, Howard found himself clinging to his attaché case. It appeared to possess some hitherto unknown buoyancy properties. His ears were ringing with the swish of the waves against the case. It was pitch black and he could see nothing. The water was as cold. His whole body felt numb, with the exception of his head, which felt like it had been placed in a cement mixer. After calling out for half an hour and getting no reply, Howard started to worry. He had never experienced such isolation.

He was beginning to lose consciousness, when he became aware that his legs appeared to be trapped and he had stopped drifting. They scrapped along the hard surface and Howard realised that the tide had guided him onto some form of solid land. Making a supreme effort, he clambered out of the sea using his two tree-like limbs and collapsed face down on the soft, wet sand.

Dawn crept in and as Howard looked around he could see

the beach had isolated pieces of debris, presumably washed up from the crash. Two seats sat incongruously next to each other in splendid isolation, as if forming a row, surrounded by blankets, rucksacks and small suitcases. Further from the beach, partially blocking the view to the horizon, was a large piece of fuselage, emblazoned with the airline logo. Fortunately, as far as he could see, there did not appear to be any bodies, or perhaps worse body parts. He had been dreading this sight.

Already he could feel the increasing strength of the early morning sun and he laid everything other than his underwear out on the beach to dry. Opening the case, it was clear after a few minutes that the laptop did not currently work and he placed this by the clothes, in the vain hope that it would dry off in the sun and spark into life later. Howard smiled to himself; no such problem with the radio. He placed it in direct sunlight, switched it on and soon the spoken word was drifting across the beach.

He listened intently to the news, the weather and the sport- there was a Test Match taking place with England playing the West Indies. The plane crash was mentioned. His spirits rose as he heard they had located some wreckage and were searching a large area of the Caribbean. Looking around he could see that there was an abundance of fruit hanging from several types of tree. After making a shelter for the evening and locating some food to eat Howard laid back listening on the now dry sand. At least he had some form of window on the world beyond the island. He also felt a sense of satisfaction that he was experiencing the usefulness of the radio at first hand.

After about an hour the radio emitted a final sudden bleep and then stopped working. It took Howard less than a minute to locate the problem. The cost cutting they had carried out to reduce the radio price had resulted in a cheaper, now clearly sub-standard, battery being used to store the solar energy. Carefully he took the radio to pieces, arranging them on his jacket so as to avoid any damage from the sand on the beach. Then painstakingly he cleaned each component and carefully reassembled them, a task he had done many times in his laboratory back at the university.

After two further hours it was evident that the radio could not be made to function and appeared beyond repair. Howard was distraught. His annoyance at being relieved of his access to the outside world was compounded by the realisation that he was the name behind the brand. He started to wonder if this had happened to the other radios they sold.

xxx

Three weeks past. Howard had descended into a morose mood fairly soon after that first horrendous day, mainly because there were no further events of any note. Each day the sun rose. Each day the tide crawled eagerly up the beach and then slumped slowly back again, like a listless diabetic. There was an abundant supply of fruit, hanging low on the bushes and trees. The climate this time of year was warm, so he never had to make a fire for warmth. Howard managed to catch and kill a range of flat fish, and using sea salt he cured these raw and ate them several days later. The shelter he had made was useful to keep the large flying insects away as he slept, but there was no need to use it to keep warm or dry. He used coconut oil on his hair and skin and washed his clothes regularly in the sea water, drying them like tobacco leaves on a makeshift rack made from wicker-like branches.

The first class lifestyle he had enjoyed in the past and had envisaged for this trip was now a distant memory. How he longed for the easy, casual intellectual chat he had enjoyed on almost any topic with his peers and friends back in his old life. He now realised that those social evenings at the theatre, restaurant or pub had been taken for granted. Now time dragged as each day became an endless repetition of the last. Even more so because he knew the radio would have made the experience more bearable.

When the rescue came it was all over very quickly. The plane flew over mid morning and after midday he saw a large boat appear on the horizon. Then a smaller launch came up the beach and the coastguard soon had him back on the main boat. Several hours afterwards it docked at an inhabited island that possessed a grass runway. The weekly flight back to Brazil was scheduled for the next day and Howard began to feel remarkably upbeat.

After a shower at the only makeshift hotel, he enjoyed his first balanced meal for several months of fried chicken and chips, together with some local vegetables. Each mouthful made his realise how far he had been from civilisation on his improvised diet. Later he took a late evening walk around the only town before turning in for the night. Away from the hotel he could see that the island was very poor, most of the people appeared to live in flimsy shacks with tin roofs. Apparently, this because the regular hurricane threat meant there was little point building anything too permanent. Consequently, most had no electricity or running water. In fact, it had been the focus of a humanitarian aid campaign overseen from the UK.

He turned the corner to see a small local food store was still open. He purchased a can of fizzy drink and gulped it down, quenching his thirst in the hot evening air. By the side of the road was a large refuse bin, which he opened to throw in the can he had just finished. Inside, to his dismay, was a pile of discarded broken Boner Solar radios.

Travelling with my drug

We headed the car southwards and within a couple of hours we were approaching the Gulf. The heavy rain that had sluiced down, devouring everything in its path on the highway, had stopped. Everything was newly washed and gleaming in the late afternoon sun. The town we pulled into was unlike anything we had seen on the journey, like a Surrey town back home with lawns beside the neat red brick houses. All the lawns were freshly mowed in strips and the white windows were framed by blue shutters. He pulled the MG sports car over into a small street off the main road. On the street there were seals, skipping along on their front legs, like they were doing the double Dutch on a skipping rope. Man those seals could move!

I climbed out and stretched my legs. Every so often there was a flat pelt lying beside the path on the green lawn. They looked like the skin of some kind of beaver, or maybe a racoon. To be honest I didn't want to look too hard, it wasn't pretty. Then I saw movement out of the side of my eye. A couple of gators come to join the party. I beat it back to the inside of the car pretty quickly when those bad boys started moving along the street, I can tell you!

So I suggested we move on.

'No', Cody stuttered, 'I want this filled up first and these plates cleaned.'

Anyway, I stared at the coffeemaker in the shape of a skull he was holding in his hand. It just looked wrong, but he was driving so I took it and wandered off in the opposite direction to those gators.

'The water goes in through the back of the head', he shouted after me.

Well, it was pretty much suburbia all around and nobody in the gardens to say hello to at that, let alone, 'can you clean these and add some water in here, please.' So I walked a bit further. Then just round the corner there was this massive gothic castle or chateau as they say in France. It looked out of place. Black granite rock. The whole of one side was lit up even though it was still early afternoon, so I went up to the dark part, figuring I could nip in here, find what I wanted and nobody would be any the wiser. Massive great doors, nearly twice my height, but they opened pretty easily and I was in a dark hall. Cold with a musty, damp smell; so not too inviting. I caught a glimpse of the stationary figures lined up against the walls on either side, dressed in full size coats of armour. This confused me. I didn't expect this in the states at all, maybe in the goal or town hall back in the England. Behind them, damask curtains hung covering much of the walls like giant man-made cobwebs.

I saw a little chink of light coming through the doors to

the left. I guess they led into some sort of banqueting room.
As I opened the doors, what struck me was how could so
many people make so little noise? Mind you they were old,
very old. In fact, some might have been dead. As I looked
around I couldn't see any of them move at all.

Then this maid with an expression resembling a stuffed
fish marched over to me. Pretty much everybody else in the
room was ancient and they were all seated. She was the
youngest in the room, which wasn't saying much. Her
clothes were old, but her apron was crisply ironed.

'Can I help you?' she barked, clearly intending not to help
at all.

So I told her about the coffee maker and the plates.

'Oh no, all this water,' she pointed to the rows of still and
sparkling water on the table behind her 'is needed for the
party.'

'Really?' I said. I mean, it did look like a lot of water. It
didn't look much like a party either.

'Yes' she said, as she turned her back dismissing me.

Then an old guy struggled over using some sort of
walking frame and held out his hand. He had a glass eye that
looked at the maid, making her jump. He looked at me with
his good eye, raising its eyebrow as he did.

'Felix McGinn, son. My party. Let him have some.' He
gestured magnanimously to the array of glass containers.
Well I mean it was kind and all that, but it was only water! So

176

I nodded a polite thanks.

So she filled the coffeemaker, at the back of the head, even though she looked like she been asked to wipe out a drain. They even cleaned the plates. Once that was done I beat it out of there pretty quickly. Strangely as soon as I was out of the room, I heard bolts slide across and a key turn in the lock; I mean let's be honest, why would I want to go back inside anyway?

xxx

Trouble was I couldn't find the way back at all. Opening the front doors everything was now draped in a thick mist. Blindly, I stumbled out into the great unknown. I could see nothing. I could hear the raucous barking of a pack of dogs apparently in the near vicinity, which immediately made me feel uneasy, so I moved off quickly.

I began to pick up the strong whiff of cannabis. By a small green I saw a short dark man, with what looked like a turban on his head, smoking a ridiculously large joint emerging from behind a copse of willow trees.

'Forget the west man, the east is best, the east is best' he mumbled when he registered my presence. And then in a less philosophical vein 'Yo, peace man!'

Then I saw he was holding a leash, which was attached to a dog collar. Wearing it was a man, naked and walking on all fours. This man bared his teeth; the incisors were overly large and prominent- as if they had been sharpened deliberately for effect. Traces of dribble were visible in the stubble at the side of his mouth.

'Don't worry about Martyn. He's an accountant!'

With that the man-dog sat on his haunches and defecated onto the grass. The small man got out a dog pooh bag and attempted to pick up the large brown mess.

'Got to go. I've only got one bag and he usually wants to go twice', he said, turning abruptly on his heels and scuttled off. Still on all fours, Martyn turned back as he was walking away and barred the incisors in my direction, letting out a menacing snarl.

I decided to hot foot it off. When I got back Cody was waiting by the car. There was no sign of the seals or alligators.

'Great' he said 'Hot coffee!'

Well, of course we had an argument then about the fact I hadn't plugged it in. I had to get into the MG cradling it on my lap, while he continued to rant at me. That was a tight squeeze in the passenger seat. He pointed the bonnet south and insisted on a wheel spin so, of course, I banged my head, hard. Suddenly there was a bolt of lightning, a loud clap of thunder and the heavens opened as it poured down with heavy metallic rain.

'God, that hurt!' I said as I woke up. I sure travelled to a lot of places with the drug that my doctor was prescribing!

Lotto

A s the dusk began to settle on the Santander shoreline, Juan moved slowly along the grand promenade, making his way past the ferry terminal, towards the traditional Spanish facades that housed the bars, hotels and restaurants. It really was a beguiling sight as the lights burned brightly like fireflies in the dusk, illuminating the buildings with soft back lighting. Under one armpit he wedged his wooden crutch and over his other shoulder he carried his regulation issue Lotto seller satchel. His weaker leg, withered by polio, dragged behind him as the crossed the main seafront road and climbed on to the pavement. His usual location was outside a lively tapas bar, popular with locals. He had learnt to avoid foreign tourist locations as they never wanted to purchase lotto tickets.

As he arrived now, Alejandro, one of the owners waved to him and gestured that they would make him a coffee. Although his living accommodation was sparse and he had little money, accreditation as an official Lotto seller meant that he was accepted by the local businesses. He always made an effort to look smart which also endeared him to the bar owners. Today he wore a smart fake pink Ralph Lauren polo shirt, his old stonewashed Pepe jeans and a pair of tattered brown leather loafers. During the summer months he started work at about eight o'clock each evening and usually packed up about three o'clock in the morning when only the night clubbers were still out and about, most of their change spent. Alejandro handed him a fresh hot coffee and a cinnamon pastry. He propped his crutch against the pillar on the outside of the shop and arranged his leather satchel, ready to sell the tickets. He had a small placard that stood beside him with the Lotto logo to confirm his licensed accreditation. Then he leaned back and ate the pastry, whilst sipping on the hot drink.

Business had been very slow this last week. Normally he would have been worried. However, the promise of the biggest payout of the year as a result of a rollover for unclaimed prizes for the last four weeks put Juan in a positive frame of mind. The next draw was tomorrow morning and tonight was the last opportunity to purchase tickets. There was a palpable sense of anticipation in the air across all of Spain. TV adverts and newspapers run headlines reminding people to buy tickets for "The big one!"

The slow dribble of early evening diners began to increase as the sun set after nine o'clock. Checking his tabs several times, Juan was alarmed to find he had still only sold nine tickets. This was not the increase in trade he had expected. A bar over the road was showing a La Ligue football match and having reached the interval was now blasting out the adverts, including one mentioning the Lotto rollover. Juan smiled to himself, hopefully this would do the trick.

Sure enough, a few seconds later a group of young men rushed out and purchased ten tickets between them. Then a couple leaving another restaurant saw this and came over to purchase a further four. By two thirty in the morning when Juan was packing up it was the most successful night he could remember, selling over three hundred tickets. As always, he made sure he had all the stubs in the inner packet of the satchel. Each night he handed these into the Lotto office in the town centre as he made his way home. Just as he had hitched his crutch under his arm a glamorous middle aged couple who were the last to leave the tapas bar came over. Juan wanted to go now, but the man was persistent so he quickly handed over a run of ten tickets.

The couple were around the corner before he realised that having taken the money for the ten tickets he had only handed over nine. One was left in the booklet. He called urgently after them, but the noise from the local nightclub and bars drowned his words. He would never catch up with them. Instead he packed up and made his way home, dropping off all the tabs into the office. He kept the sole ticket in his pocket.

xxx

The next day, like many of the other Lotto sellers Juan

went to his local cafe to hear the winning numbers for the rollover. The atmosphere was thick with smoke and smelt of fresh aftershave, cigarettes and beer. Everybody watched with anticipation the announcement on the large wall mounted TV. When the numbers appeared he felt sick to the base of his stomach- they were the numbers on his ticket. To make it worse, the presenter on the national TV show said that the winning ticket was sold in Santander.

He looked in his wallet. The ticket was still there! Juan felt the sweat cascade down his back under his shirt as the sellers discussed who could have sold the ticket. He quickly crept out of the bar.

'Stop' a voice called. He turned to see Gabriella, a gangly brunette running after him. 'What's the matter?'

'I can't believe it.' He told her. 'Last night a man bought ten tickets just as I was packing up. I pulled off the run of tickets and took the money. And then after he'd gone I realised that I still had one of them with the stubs.'

'And that was the winning ticket!' Gabriella finished off.

He nodded sadly. 'He must know that I have the ticket as he is one short and he is one away from the winning number.'

'Why worry, you can claim it and be a millionaire?'

'No. I can't. I need to find him and give him the ticket.'

'Are you crazy? This is your lucky break. This is what we all dream of. You can leave this life behind forever.'

But Juan shook his head. 'I just have to.'

'Man, you're mad! But you're secret is safe with me.' Gabriella shrugged her shoulders and wandered back to the bar.

'Thanks!' he called after her.

Walking back to his room, Juan began to ponder. Was this the right decision or should he have listened to Gabriella?

Back in his bed Juan lay awake in the humid air, turning his predicament over in his mind. He remembered the stories his grandmother told him as he sat on her knee when he was young. That was before both her and his parents died. His world had been turned upside down in under a year. But he thought back to the stories. He knew what was good and what was not good. The stories had she had told him taught him that. His mind was decided, he could not take the ticket, he knew it was not his and he knew it had to be handed back to its rightful owner.

And so Juan set about locating the buyer of the ticket. The next morning he went back to the tapas bar and eventually using payment receipts and the reservation book, they managed to identify the name of the man. He found the address from the internet and made his way to the imposing house in the middle class suburb of Santander. This was clearly a wealthy area, with expensive cars in the driveways. He halted. Did they need the money?

Shaking off the thought and reminding himself he had made his decision he approached the house. After ringing the bell, he patiently waited. Eventually, a woman he recognised from the evening answered the door. She looked at him suspiciously.

'Who are you? What do you want? I won't buy any of your goods!'

He explained about the ticket. They had won. He handed it over and informed her how to claim the Lotto rollover.

xxx

Next day Juan was in his usual place at the nine o'clock. Time had dragged and business was very slow. Now the rollover had been claimed, the Lotto prize was relatively small. He set up his placard and arranged his satchel with the new strips of tickets. Back to usual, he thought to himself. Juan sipped on his coffee and scanned the street for possible sales.

Just then a car drew up. An expensive German car; he thought it was a Mercedes. Juan looked at it admiringly. A sharply dressed man who he recognised climbed out and walked around to him.

'I just wanted to say thank you.' He held out his hand.

'No problem. Nice car by the way.' Juan replied.

'The car is for you. A present. A thank you!'

'Really! That is very kind of you. You'd don't have to do

that.' He was shocked by the generosity.

'Yes, but you didn't have to give me the ticket back. That was kind. You had little money and could have kept it for yourself. '

Water welled in Juan's eyes. 'Thank you.' He said, choking back the tears. 'Thank you so very much.'

'No thank you for your honesty,' the man said, as he threw Juan the car keys.

Ten minutes later and there was a loud honk outside the small tapas bar. Lazily, Gabriella raised her head from the table where she had been sitting, cradling a near finished coffee. Her eyes widened as she saw her friend waving from the front seat of the Mercedes convertible. Then she ran outside, waving frantically.

The Comfort Station

The road narrowed as we passed the Coniston sign that thanked me for driving carefully and then turned tightly to the right up a single lane flanked by dry stone walls that enclosed the sheep filled fields. Our old people mover groaned as I shifted down to second gear and negotiated the potholed track that took us further and further away from civilisation.

'How far away was that pub?' my husband Geoff sighed twenty minutes later, as we began to drive through a small glade of trees.

'About three miles, a good walk. We can do it tomorrow lunchtime.' I said positively.

'Okay.' He nodded, and after a minute or so. 'Here we are!'

We pulled into a small drive beside the isolated cottage, gleaming with white-washed stone walls. The symmetry of the door and windows was complimented by the lilac flowering wisteria which crawled lazily up the facade. Stepping out of the car, the bucolic views were so breathtaking it took us all a few moments to regain our composure. The low vale spread out before us, the bright green grass ribbed by the criss-cross of the stone walls and small becks, before climbing a steep escarpment to the tor topped peak. To one side was a small copse of oak and beech trees. There was no sign of any other building and the large garden was surrounded by fields as far as the eye could see.

'Complete peace and quiet.' I cried, waving my finger at him.

'Yep, you can't deny that!' He admitted, raising his eyebrows.

'Oh come on. You know the last two times we went away you moaned about the noise through the walls from next door, the noise coming from the next door garden or stressed over the issue of car parking. None of that. Just us and the girls. Peace and quiet.'

He nodded. He knew I was right.

We had made good time from our village in the West Midlands, and once unpacked, we all settled in the garden on the rustic furniture provided to enjoy the view. Mid July is not always great in the Lakes, but this was a beautiful day and we were not going to waste it. The girls were happy sharing the swing and trampoline that basked in a suntrap spot on the lawn.

'Right, who's for a cuppa?'

Hands shot up from the three of them and I was despatched to the small kitchen to put the kettle on. Pretty basic I had to admit, but it had all the appliances, even if it was cramped and appeared to have a couple of overloaded plug sockets. Tiles were everywhere; on the floor and walls, there were even polystyrene seventies ones on the ceiling. Tagging onto the back of the kitchen was a small bathroom. I remembered, with some annoyance, that the details stated there was only one toilet; so this was it. Looking inside I realised there was barely space to swing a cat. The bath appeared to be three quarter size, which would not please my six foot, rugby playing husband.

Better keep that surprise for later I thought, returning to the kitchen to switch on the kettle and taking in the fantastic view from its small window. Just as I was turning away, I spotted a small movement in the near distance. Looking again more closely, I could pick out a couple of ramblers who appeared to be on a footpath travelling diagonally down the hillside.

From the back of a cupboard, I managed to locate a fairly utilitarian-looking teapot, together with a matching white milk jug and cups and saucers. Once the tea was brewed I set up a tray. I returned to the garden, only to see the ramblers walking along the footpath which appeared to run along the bottom of the garden.

'Hi. Lovely day!' a tall woman in her sixties waved as her head moved along the top the hedge. Beside her, the companion nodded her consent.

'Bloody Hell, Great! Talk about privacy.' Geoff muttered and slumped into the sun lounger.

'Look it's pretty remote. I can't believe many people take this path. They're probably the only ones we'll see during the whole week.' I said. Geoff raised his eyebrows.

The girls seemed happy enough exploring the outside area and Geoff finally calmed down enough to remind me that I had not brought any cake or biscuits to munch with our tea.

'Don't worry. I'll get them myself' he muttered pseudo generously, launching himself up from the chair and ambling up the stone path.

Less than two minutes later he was back, and not with the biscuits.

'I don't bloody believe it!'

'What?'

'Those bloody ramblers are using our loo!'

'What, don't be ridiculous.'

'I am not being ridiculous. I just went to nip to the toilet before getting the chocolate digestives, only to be told by that old biddy we just spoke to that her friend was in the bloody toilet and she was next in the queue!'

'Right!' I marched up the garden with Geoff in my wake. As I entered one of the elderly women in walking boots was coming out of the toilet accompanied by the sound of a flushing cistern, as the other started to enter. I held the door and stood in her way.

'Excuse me, I am not sure what you think you are doing, but we have rented this cottage for the next week. This is our toilet. Please can you leave now?'

'I am sorry, but it says on our guide that this is the public convenience we are able to use. Look it is marked on this map.' She held a small Lakeland guide- labelled "Walk No 5 - The Old Man of Coniston."' As I examined the map I could make out the footpath and then at a location which was clearly our cottage, a small red circle containing the letters WC. I looked at the guide and passed it to Geoff.

'I will have to get on to them tomorrow. This is a rental property so there is clearly some mistake.'

'Well apologies all round. Can Maureen just use the toilet and we'll be out of your hair?' said the woman who had come out of the toilet earlier. I nodded and we both retreated to the sanctity of the garden.

'Great!' Geoff thundered.

'Don't worry. I'll ring Lakeland cottages first thing tomorrow as soon as they open and sort it. Better still we can drive to their office in Ambleside.' I sighed.

xxx

Several hours later after a hastily prepared evening meal from the provisions we had unpacked, I drew the curtains as dusk closed in. The girls had organised their bedroom, having fought over the top bunk. Both beds were now festooned with possessions and Geoff and I decided, for tonight at least, to grant it exclusion zone status. Downstairs in the lounge all was silent and Geoff was ensconced in The Telegraph crossword in an old leather chair by the small inglenook. I smiled when I saw how relaxed he was now compared to earlier. I put my glass of rose next to his bottle of Old Gnasher on the small coffee table and settled down with the Saturday magazine supplement.

I must have drifted off after the journey, when I was woken by the sound of talking and a loud belch. I checked my watch and it was just after ten o'clock. Geoff was still dozing in the chair, so leaving the small sitting room I walked into the kitchen and opened the back door. At first I thought it was a solar light that came on automatically in the near darkness, but as I walked towards the talking I could see it moving. It was a torch.

'Hi!' A guy his early twenties smiled over. 'We pitched our tent a little way down the garden to give you privacy, but not too far so we can't use the loo.'

As he spoke another guy with a shaved head appeared from the tent holding two cans of lager and sporting a massive "Motorhead" tattoo across his chest. His appearance was accompanied by another loud belch.

'Cheers, love!' he held up his can and winked, passing the second can to the other man.

'Piss off. Now!'

I turned to see an enraged Geoff, now fully awake,

standing behind me glaring at the two men.

'No hang on! We can stay here. It says so in our walking guide.'

'We know that. We have already had that conversation. We are contacting the agency tomorrow. It's a mistake.' I said patiently.

'Bollocks! We're not moving. We spent an hour putting this up.' The first guy said, not so pleasantly at all now. 'And I'm off for a dump in that toilet. The curry we had earlier at that pub has gone right through me.'

'I'm coming as well, Tony.' A blonde girl with an upper class accent in a skimpy top climbed out of the tent and followed him up the garden.

'Oh no you don't!' Geoff launched himself into their path, blocking the way.

'Oh yeah?' Said the young man angrily.

It looked like it was going to get nasty, so reluctantly I decided that there was only one course of action.

'Right, I'll settle this once and for all. I'm phoning the police.'

There was an uneasy stand off as we all stood in the garden, waiting. I calmed the girls down after they had witnessed the scene from the upstairs back bedroom window. Geoff steadfastly refused any access to the toilet.

xxx

Twenty minutes later, a small marked police car rolled silently up and parked in front of the cottage.

'This will be an end to it!' Geoff muttered under his breath.

'Don't think so mate!' Laughed the bald guy, as he rocked backwards and forwards in an agitated state.

'Now then madam, I believe you called us regarding intruders on the property.' said a young policeman.

'Yes. Please can you explain to these people that we are renting this property and that, despite what their rambling guide says, they cannot camp here or use the toilet facilities.'

'Well. I'm afraid they are correct. There is an old bylaw in the area due to the remoteness of your location. Because of its unique position this cottage is the only dwelling in this area with running water. As such it is defined as a comfort station. That means it should provide toilet facilities to any travellers that are in need in the area.'

'Right, I'm in that loo. Excuse me!' The man now pushed past Geoff triumphantly and headed indoors to use the toilet.'

'That's it. They can use the loo and then piss off.' Geoff growled.

'Sorry mate we're staying!' the bald guy chipped in.

Geoff lunged towards him, but the policeman intervened.

'I am sorry sir, he's correct.' He said, holding a hand up in Geoff's face. 'The back garden of this cottage is often used by hikers if they can't find anywhere else to safely camp. I'm afraid it's written in a covenant.'

I turned to Geoff, but he was already getting the girls into the car and disappeared back into the cottage. Moments later he returned, laid down with our cases, which were wedged shut with items trailing from them as he stomped over to the car.

'Geoff!'

'It's sorted. I've booked us into that pub down the road.'

The Inspection

Pete rearranged the lightweight silver chairs in groups of four around the small metal tables. It was just after ten thirty on a Friday and the two groups who had been eating breakfast there had just left. Whistling, he took a long drag on his cigarette and a swig of his now cold coffee. The kiosk had been open now for nearly an hour and the crisp spring sunshine that lit that morning had caused a small influx of visitors to the picturesque bay, nestling under the imposing white cliffs. He had only finished touching up the paint around the serving hatch last week and stood back to admire his work. The sea shimmered like a mirror and dog walkers and joggers weaved their ways along the coastal paths and short promenade that overlooked the pebble beach and rock pools.

The small car park held three cars and a blue van. Several seagulls had descended near to the large wheelie bin at the back of the kiosk, eagerly surveying for the rich pickings they could smell from within it. Pete marched over and aimed a stone skillfully at the bin, the sound enough to move them on their way to another location. Another day in paradise, he thought to himself. The idea to leave the rat race and start this small business certainly seemed like the right one.

A middle-aged man wearing loose fitting suit trousers and

a navy cagoule was approaching the kiosk. He had a somewhat pompous air.

'What can I get you?' Mary smiled out from the serving hatch.

'I've come to do an inspection.' He replied brusquely as he peered beyond her into the kiosk.

She saw that the man held a clipboard in his hand. It appeared to have several official pages attached under a thick silver clip. He was now chewing the end of a blue biro, whilst staring back at Mary.

'Okay. We weren't expecting a visit. Pete, can you come over here a minute?'

'Sure.' Pete wandered back from the edge of the seating area, where he had been arranging the kiosk sign and cleaning the smaller rubbish bin, used by customers. Seeing the man, he nodded acknowledgement, flicking his cigarette butt into the bin.

'Hi, What's up?' said Pete, smiling at the stranger.

'This gentleman tells me that he is here to carry out an investigation.'

'Really? Well that's news to us. We had one only six months ago. Matt came down and spent a morning with us. He wrote up the report and gave us a clean bill of health. Do you know Matt?'

'No I don't know Matt.' The man shook his head.

'That's strange? He's being doing our local council

inspections ever since we started five years ago. Anyway, what's it for?'

'Food hygiene.' The man appeared to quote from the clipboard. 'And health and safety. I'll need to come into the kiosk.' He added.

They gestured to the side door and the man entered the ten foot square space. It was a tight squeeze for two people, so Pete stayed outside. Once inside the kiosk at first the man seemed a little bewildered by the densely stocked shelves, but soon appeared to regain his composure.

'Hot drinks?' he gestured inquiringly to the large machine against the far wall.

Mary spent the next ten minutes taking him through all the drink combinations that the kiosk offered. Finally she showed him where the milk was kept in the small fridge.

'Almond, oat and soya milk?' he asked.

'Only soya milk. We don't offer oat or almond.' Pete called through the hatch from outside. 'We can't cope with all these different options.'

'Oh dear, that's most disappointing. They are very popular nowadays. I always take almond milk myself.' The man sucked in air between his teeth and made a tutting noise. He appeared to place a large cross on the sheet he held.

'Is it a problem?' Mary looked alarmingly at the clipboard. 'Will it affect the result of the inspection?'

'It's not great really, is it?' was the dismissive reply.

'Pete. Get on to Rory. See if we can get some oat and almond milk down here?'

Pete raised his eyebrows and shrugged his shoulders. He was getting a little annoyed by this over zealousness and he was still not convinced this was an official visit.

'Yeah. Rory. Pete here. Can you get some oat milk and almond milk down to us as soon as possible? Thanks Rory.' He hung up and nodded to the man and Mary. 'It's on its way.'

'It's not on your menu.' The man pointed to the large font on the board displayed on the front of the kiosk beside the serving hatch.

'Jesus!' Pete muttered under his breath. He looked around and found a black board marker pen. Leaning across and apologising to customers queuing to be served, he slowly added the extra two milk options to the menu. The man now seemed happy enough.

'Now, let's look at the food preparation area. This is the main grill?'

'Yes, we have a full griddle. We use this and the toasted sandwich maker.'

There were currently several burgers, bacon rashers and eggs cooking on the griddle. Mary moved over to the worktops and surreptitiously brushed some of the breadcrumbs and bacon rind from the last order into her hand and then dropped them into the bin. But the man was now looking intently at the plug socket in the corner beyond the griddle, which had three leads coming out of an extension socket.

'That won't pass. You need another lead off that socket there.' He pointed to a socket in the far corner that just had one lead to a small kettle. 'You need that to have another lead on it to spread the load. Have you got another extension lead?'

'Now hang on!' Pete glared at him. 'We have never had any issues with the set up in previous inspections.'

'No Pete. Ring Rory now, please.'

'Jesus, for Christ's sake!' Pete was near exploding. 'Rory. Sorry mate, it's me again. We need another five metre extension lead as well. As soon as. Thanks mate.'

'Great- I'm half way down to the bay. Now I'll have to drive back to the DIY superstore on the ring road! Why couldn't you have told me earlier?' Rory was beginning to sound exasperated.

Pete dropped down into a chair and gestured angrily behind the man's back. This was turning into a nightmare. There was now a small queue of customers that Mary was serving whilst this was all going on and a few of them had begun to look over towards the man. Two women started talking pointedly about the importance of good food hygiene in a way which began to get Pete's hackles up. Another customer started searching for a logo showing the kiosk food hygiene rating.

About ten minutes later a small battered white van shot down the road into the car park and skidded to a sharp halt at the side of the kiosk, engulfing Pete and the customers in a light cloud of dust. Shortly afterwards, Mary handed the man a latte with almond milk, which he inspected carefully and then began to slowly sip, rather loudly.

'Well, I think everything now seems to be in order now.' The man said suddenly, as he looked out of the hatch, quickly stepping out into the car park.

At that moment, a young man who had been standing at the corner of the car park, about twenty feet away from the kiosk raised his thumb.

'It's a wrap mate!'

'Hang on' Pete called angrily over. 'What's this?'

But by this time the man had reached the small blue van. He removed his jacket and ruffled his hair. The open sliding door of the van revealed an array of cameras and microphones. As Pete jogged over the door slid shut and the van started to pull off.

'Hey!' Pete banged on the passenger door.

The window was lowered several inches and the man who had played the role of the inspector smiled back at him. Pete saw he was much younger now he had ditched his disguise.

'Thanks mate!' the man grinned. 'You were great. I mean, you got really wound up! It's all recorded now. Watch out for the TV programme- Caught on Crazy Camera!'

He made a clicking gesture with his fingers, as if taking a photo. With that the van sped out of the car park and up the hill, accompanied by the sound of loud laughter.

Acknowledgements

Firstly, thank you to Sarah for her constant encouragement and support over the years and to Beth and Laura for their help and advice. A big thank you to Andy and Claudia for their proof-reading- an exhaustive task! Finally, thank you to my mother for instilling a lifelong love of reading in me from an early age.

The criticism from my fellow students on the Oxford University Fiction Writing course has been invaluable and the feedback from the course tutor, the author Gareth Dickson, has definitely made me a better writer.

All characters in these stories are completely fictitious and all resemblance to persons living or dead is purely coincidental. All real locations have been researched by myself and any factual errors are purely my own.

Printed in Great Britain
by Amazon